I0677516

THE ECOLOG

**Wildside Press Books
by Ray Faraday Nelson**

Dog-Headed Death
The Ecolog
Then Beggars Could Ride
TimeQuest

THE ECOLOG

by Ray Faraday Nelson

WILDSIDE PRESS
BERKELEY HEIGHTS • NEW JERSEY

THE ECOLOG

This book is copyright © 1977 by R.F. Nelson. All rights reserved. No portion of this book may be reprinted without obtaining the prior written consent of the publisher, except for brief passages quoted for review purposes. For more information, contact: Wildside Press, P.O. Box 45, Gillette, NJ 07933-0045.

The cover design is by John Betancourt and is copyright © 2000 by Wildside Press.

First Wildside Press edition: April 2000.

INTRODUCTION

In my previous book, *Then Beggars Could Ride,* I proposed a certain kind of utopia, one that could be accomplished on a limited energy budget, one that avoided the boredom of most "perfect societies" by decentralization and diversification, by making room for many different ways of life rather than attempting to impose a single lifestyle on everyone.

Some of the helpful souls who hear my novels read out loud, chapter by chapter, before publication pointed out that my planet wasn't very "far out." It was still the planet Earth, even if an Earth set in the future. They wondered if such a society would be possible on another planet.

This was an embarrassing question, since it exposed one of my worst blind spots. I knew something about history, the arts, mythology and other such "humanities," as one might expect from a graduate of the Hutchins' Era University of Chicago, but unfortunately I knew absolutely nothing about astronomy.

My friends reassured me that many science fiction writers were in the same boat, even some of the all-time greats. Ray Bradbury, they said, created a Mars that, even at the time of his writing, was impossible. And what did Philip K. Dick know about the stars? Or Edgar Rice Burroughs? Or Reg Bretnor? Or Harlan Ellison? Or Mike Moorcock? If ignorance was bliss for all these giants, why should a small fry like me worry my poor head about such things?

They had a point, but I was worried all the same.

For years I'd been writing science fiction and, as they pointed out, had almost never ventured off the surface of homey old Sol Three. I was limited, and I don't like to be limited.

I decided to give myself a crash course in astronomy and have a go at writing my first true space-opera.

I laid my problem before Poul Anderson. He helpfully provided me with a xerox of an article he wrote for the November 1966 issue of *The Bulletin of the Science Fiction Writers of America* entitled "How to Build a Planet." I read it, but I must admit I did not understand it. I read it again. A pattern began to emerge. It made my head ache, but it certainly revived my flagging sense of wonder.

I talked to another friend of mine, amateur astronomer and cat collector Leonard Metula, who loaned me a few books: *Alone in the Universe* by John Macvey; *Intelligence in the Universe* by MacGowan and Ordway; and *Superworlds* by Joshua Strickland. These too were a bit steep for me.

The breakthrough came when the teenage girl next door lent me her highschool astronomy text. With a painful sensation of inferiority, I browsed through it. From that moment on there was no turning back.

Astronomy was one subject I was going to understand if it killed me. Help came from many sources. Robert Anton Wilson patiently explained black holes, which he said might be the ultimate reality. Astrologer Richard Fabry drew up my horoscope. I watched Star Trek reruns. I searched everywhere for a map of the Milky Way Galaxy and finally, in a war game called "Alpha Centauri," found a remarkable chart of at least the neighboring stars. At the "Federation Outpost" on Telegraph Avenue in Berkeley I located a relentlessly authentic starchart of the skies of Vulcan, where Mr. Spock comes from. I read *The Mote in God's Eye* by Niven and Pournelle and was very impressed until, in a *Galaxy* article, the authors admitted fudging. (Their spaceship was built from a plastic model kit.)

Gradually, bit by bit, a grand panorama began to unfold. There were population-one stars located in the spiral arms of our galaxy, and there were population-two stars located in the hub of the galaxy and in galactic clusters above and below the galactic plane. Population-two stars were short of heavy elements and might not have any planets, or perhaps only gaseous ones. Double and triple stars might also lack planets. But there were still many possible planetary systems left, particularly since planets have been recently discovered around two nearby stars.

I was annoyed about that. Here I sit in front of my television set every night under the delusion that I'm watching the news, and all the time whole planets are being discovered without the media breathing a word about it. In case you too haven't heard, there are perhaps two planets circling Barnard's Star about six light-years from here; and around Lalande 21185, about eight point two light-years away, swings a monster planet ten times the mass of Jupiter.

If there are that many planets here in our own neighborhood, that means that (a) there are lots and lots of planets all over the place, or (b) we live in a very exclusive neighborhood.

Thus encouraged, I set about planning the book you now hold in your hands.

If you wonder where I found the wild descriptions of flight at near light speeds, I did not just make them up. They are borrowed from *Spaceflight*, the usually quite conservative journal of the British Interplanetary Society.

The planet itself, New Earth, is my own creation.

It's a lot like Old Earth, but it has arrived at this appearance by quite a different route. The star it rotates around is a population-two star, which means any planets it spawns must be very low on metals. I like it that way, since this makes particularly pressing the problems of ecological poverty I want to portray. New Earth has been artificially made to resemble Old Earth, but the problem of the shortage of raw materials has not been licked.

Before I asked the question, "Can we have utopia on a budget?"

Now I ask, "Can we have utopia on a very tight budget?"

The answer, it seems to me, is that when the available

resources fall below a certain point utopia is still possible, but only for a tiny minority. I don't go into it much in this book, but it also seems to me that the form of government is largely determined by the availability of resources. Primitive technology is unable to tap more than a small fraction of the available resources; for all practical purposes primitive societies operate in a condition of great scarcity and thus literally cannot afford "liberty, equality and fraternity." Authoritarian societies are the unavoidable result of extreme scarcity; conversely, democratic forms of government are dependent on a certain minimum supply of energy and raw materials.

The Ecolog owes something to Pournelle and Niven; in the same article where they admit to the use of plastic model spaceships, they outline their reasons for using an aristocratic style of government in *God's Eye*. I think they used an aristocratic style of government because that is the life-style they secretly long for, though they are fair enough to admit the great unsolved problem of aristocracy: "How to avoid succession crisis?"

When the Man on Horseback dies, how do we avoid having everything fall apart, as it did on the death of, say, Alexander the Great? My *Ecolog* solves this problem in a way I believe to be scientifically possible, but I also show, I hope, how scientific factors are not the only ones in play. Is it really such a good idea to have a Man on Horseback—or in my case a Woman on Horseback—who lasts forever?

In the early stages, the spaceship was called *The Victoria,* but then I changed it to *The Corregidor.* My hero, Commodore Briggs, does represent the values of the Victorian Age, but I didn't want to give the impression that determination, self-discipline, a sense of duty and a feeling for elegance died, with the Grand Old Monarch Victoria, at 6:30 p.m., January 22, 1901.

CHAPTER 1

"Looks like an ambush," the bow watch reported, and even through his headphones Phillips could hear restrained tension in the voice. "Two Lorn starships coming in fast at grid 12 and 12."

Dead ahead, thought Phillips. When a ship comes in at near light speed, there's no way it can be seen or detected until it's almost on top of you. Typical Lorn tactics. Strike hard and fast and kill everybody. The Lorns weren't humans, and human life meant nothing to them. *They don't even hate us. They just want us out of the way so they can have our planets.*

Another voice crackled in the headphones. "Briggs here. We'll take evasive action on computer control. Key in all battle stations and prepare to fire. On my signal we're going off manuals. Repeat, off manuals."

On manual control from the forward control room, the starship *Corregidor* began to turn.

"Now," came the voice of Commodore Briggs. On the control panel of Lieutenant Mike Phillips the little red light indicating manual control went out. The computer had taken over. Mike leaned back in his bucket seat and permitted himself a glance through the transparent canopy above him, instinctively expecting to see some sign of the enemy, though he knew they were still too far away for visual contact. There were stars in plenty; the Milky Way looked much the same as it would have from Earth, at least to the casual glance, but the nearest star was yellow orange Epsilon Eridani, a point of light behind him. Two days ago the *Corregidor* had been in orbit around her titanic fifth planet, unloading supplies for the Eridani orbiter. Mike wished he was back there now. They might have received some help from the orbiter. From here a radio message would take hours to reach friendly human ears.

The earphones crackled again. "Bow watch reporting. They're closing on us, firing." The voice was calm, almost bored, except for a faint undertone of panic.

A violent explosion shook the *Corregidor* throughout its half-kilometer length. Phillips, in the secondary control room amidships, waited for the *Corregidor* to return fire, to hit back. It was up to the computer now.

Precious seconds passed.

Nothing happened.

Mike scanned his control panel, saw that the manual control light had turned on again, red, unwavering. Mike spoke into his helmet microphone. "Manuals are still on, Commodore. The computer's not taking hold."

The secondary control room was dim, lit only by Epsilon Eridani behind him, the Milky Way above and the myriad tiny lights and green-glowing dials on the control panels that surrounded him. "Commodore Briggs," called Mike into his helmet phone, unable to totally conceal the anxiety in his voice. "Commodore Briggs. Answer please."

Still the commanding officer of the *Corregidor* did not reply, but a third voice came on the line. "The Lorns hit the main control room. Instruments say the hull is broken. There's no air in there." Mike recognized the voice. Ensign Peter DeCarli, head of damage control. DeCarli added, "Computer's hit, too."

Mike thought, *Briggs was in there, and all the other senior officers . . . except me.* He said aloud, "Briggs must be dead."

Nobody contradicted him.

As if in a dream Mike did what he was trained to do. "This is Lieutenant Phillips in the secondary control room. I'm taking command." His gloved fingers danced over the studs on the control console. The *Corregidor* leaped into motion.

Above him, outside the canopy, there was a silent flash

that would have blinded him if the durlite hadn't momentarily clouded, triggered by the safety eye. *Well, they almost nailed us again,* he thought, smiling faintly. It was not warm in the control room, but his coveralls were stuck to his back with sweat.

The canopy cleared. For an instant he glimpsed the enemy, two minute dots of light moving against the starry background. They didn't look dangerous somehow. Two little dots. The *Corregidor* rolled and the dots swung out of sight.

A voice in Mike's ear asked, "Do we fight or run?" It was Chief Engineer George Dutton. His voice sounded old.

To Mike the answer to this question was like the solution to a mathematical calculation: inevitable. Two against one. And the *Corregidor* was hit. No computer. *And me at the controls.*

"We run," Mike replied. "Cancel inertia."

"Inertia canceled," Dutton responded crisply, then added uncertainly, "If you're sure. . . ."

I've been at the helm for a matter of seconds and already they're questioning my orders. Mike snapped, "Accelerate to thirty-five thousand kilometers per hour and hold." From behind he could hear the rising whine of power.

"Aye, sir. Thirty-five thousand." Dutton would never disobey a direct order. Dutton went by the book, as Mike well knew.

The bow watch broke in. "They're firing again."

"We're making a right-angle turn," Mike said. "Now!" His gloved hand gestured over the console and the studs read his movements. The whine abruptly changed to a scream. Instantly the *Corregidor* was moving on a course perpendicular to its previous direction.

"Right angle completed, sir," noted Dutton. "They missed us." Behind Mike's right shoulder three bright flashes blazed in succession, then faded.

The headphones sounded again. "Aft watch reporting.

The Lorns are dead astern of us now, at grid six and six. They're turning to follow us. Oh oh. They're launching homing missiles."

Mike pulled off his gloves and wiped his sweating palms on the knees of his tan coveralls. "Damn bloodhounds! But we can outrun them."

"Outrun?" the chief engineer sounded doubtful.

Mike answered grimly, "We're taking this ship up to just under the speed of light. Now!"

There was a moment's hesitation. "Aye, sir."

The *Corregidor* lunged forward, as if eager for the race.

"Aft watch here. The missiles are speeding up with us, still tracking."

The whine of power grew higher and more frantic and Mike, frowning, thought he smelled the faint aroma of ozone. He glanced out through the canopy. There was, as yet, no sign of movement in the stars, though the ship was accelerating rapidly. As far as the eye could tell, the *Corregidor* was standing still.

Mike watched for a motion that never ceased to fascinate him. He did not have long to wait.

The stars began to move, but very slowly, and not in the direction one instinctively expected. They moved forward, as if they, too, were racing with the ship and the missiles that followed it.

The sky in the forward half of the canopy became more and more crowded with stars, while the canopy to the rear grew empty and dark.

"Aft watch here. The missiles are gaining on us."

The relative brightness of the stars changed. Those that had been bright became dark. Darker stars became bright, as different portions of their spectra shifted into visible range. They changed color. Even their shape changed, the round bright dots becoming distinctly oval, as if they were being crushed flat by some universal pressure—the same pressure that seemed to be driving them toward the front of the ship.

"Still gaining, sir." This from the aft watch.

"Have we any more power?" Mike asked.

"No, sir." Dutton's voice was tired, resigned.

The power whine was steady now, uncomfortably loud. They were moving faster, steadily faster, but there was no feeling of speed inside the ship, no sensation of acceleration.

The stars continued to edge forward, and now a consistent pattern began to emerge from the color change. Those farthest forward were turning blue; those farthest back turned dark red. Between the two extremes bands of graded color formed, until the entire sky became one majestic rainbow, dim to the rear, bright ahead.

"Still gaining, sir," whispered Mike's earphones. Mike bit his lip. The missiles were smaller, had less mass. They would also have less inertia to cancel, and thus would use less fuel.

"Dutton. How does our energy supply look?"

"At this acceleration?" the old man answered grimly. "Not good."

The stars dimmed, fading out in the red and blue portions of the "rainbow." The space behind the ship was now black; the space ahead of the ship was becoming black too, and a quarter of the way back the red band and blue band came together, squeezing the green, the yellow and the orange into oblivion.

Now there was one band: a shimmering violet.

And then, nothing. Total darkness.

The *Corregidor* was running blind.

"Aft watch here. I've lost visual contact on those missiles. Instrument contact is fading out too."

Mike couldn't see the missiles. Without light or some other electromagnetic radiation in the detectable bands, nobody could see them. But he knew they were there, gaining on him. If he slowed, they'd catch up and finish his ship. The missiles had been on a straight-line course behind him when the acceleration began. No, he couldn't see them, but they couldn't see him either. He was counting on that.

"I'm changing course," Mike announced.

Old man Dutton spoke instantly. "I'd advise against that, sir. No way of knowing where we'll end up."

Mike knew what he meant. It wasn't healthy to steer at near light speeds. The slightest course alteration without any external reference point could send you sailing unaware into the core of some particularly hot, white dwarf star.

"Any other suggestions?" Mike demanded.

Dutton did not reply.

"Then there's no other way." *We won't hit anything,* he silently reassured himself. *Like Briggs always used to say, "In space there's more nothing than anything."*

"Now." Mike gestured over the studs.

There was no sensation of movement on board—the stasis field saw to that—but Mike read from his instruments that the pattern of energy expended had caused the ship to branch off at an angle of ten degrees in the vertical plane . . . wherever that vertical plane might be.

"All right," Mike said, as much to himself as to anyone who might be listening on the intercom. "We slow down until we see the stars again."

"Aye, sir." The chief engineer sounded gloomy.

Mike activated the studs. The whine changed pitch, faded slightly, came up again to full strength. Energy was needed to slow down, exactly the same amount necessary to speed up. Elementary. But Dutton had said their energy store was limited.

The violet band of stars reappeared, faint at first, then brighter toward the forward end of the canopy. The band spread, and the central bands appeared: blue, green, yellow, orange, red. Some individual stars could be seen, bright squashed ovals scattered like confetti on the rainbow.

"Phillips to aft watch. Any sign of the missiles?"

"Aft watch here. Not a trace."

"Phillips to instrument room. Any missiles?"

"This is instruments. Relax, Mike. No missiles, no starships, no nothing within a hundred thousand kilometers." A human eye might not be able to sort out a missile from the distorted heavens around them, but the instruments could.

"We lost them," sighed Mike with relief, leaning back in his bucket seat. "Slow to a few hundred and let 'er drift."

"Aye, sir," several voices chorused.

The power whine held steady. The rainbow effect decreased. The stars lost their oval shapes and spread out, no longer appearing to bunch together ahead, but distributing themselves into a believable pattern across the vast space.

"Cutting power," came a voice. "Now."

The whine dropped in a long glissando that ended in a bass groan. Then there was silence.

Mike took a deep breath and asked, "Does anybody have any idea where we are?"

There was a pause; then someone answered wistfully, "Don't ask."

THE woman in the trance wore a band of metal around her forehead. Its wire leads meandered to a machine above the tank where she lay. Another wire connected the machine to a second band of metal around the forehead of a second woman. A platinum mask concealed her face from brows to chin, except for the slightly slanted eyeslits. The mask was decorated with precious jewels in ornate, floral patterns. The jewels glittered in the dim blue light. Through the wire the women conversed with each other.

You're troubled. Is it your dreams? queried the masked woman.

My dreams? echoed the sleeping one. *They are of you—falling, falling, falling.*

THE black-enameled, steel conference table and chairs stood on a long rectangle of simulated, inlaid wood flooring on a mountaintop. The late afternoon sun sent shadows stretching from the legs of the table and chairs to the edge of the floor; and as a hawk glided across the sky, his shadow passed quickly over the pitcher of water and cluster of glasses that sat on the tabletop.

In the west, where the sun blazed above a slowly changing mass of white cumulus clouds, snowcapped peaks rose from pine-covered valleys; in the east the sky was clear, except for a thin streamer of smoke that drifted lazily up from a log cabin on the mountainside; to the south were more mountains, and to the north lay a broad blue lake on which drifted one lone sailboat. A dog barked somewhere in the distance, and the echo reverberated faintly among the cliffs.

Just outside the floored-over area, half-hidden by scrubby and wind-twisted bushes, lay a human skull, yellowed, weathered and dirty. Ants paraded through the empty eye-sockets, but old Mr. Bones didn't seem to mind. No matter what happened, Mr. Bones went right on grinning. The ants formed a procession that led to the edge of the platform and stopped. There were no ants on the simulated wood floor, let alone on the conference table and chairs.

The wind that rustled the tops of the pines farther down the mountainside, came to a halt at the table and chairs.

Suddenly a panel slid open in the empty air. Lieutenant Mike Phillips stepped through the doorway. The panel promptly closed behind him. With an impatient frown he glanced around at the mountain landscape, then gestured.

Instantly the mountain landscape was replaced by a seascape at dawn. The waves crashed loudly on the beech . . . too loudly. Mike gestured again and the sound fell to a dull and distant murmur. "That's better," he muttered and squinted at his fingerwatch. "They're late."

As the gulls in the holovision mirage screamed somewhere far away, he crossed the room and seated himself at the head of the table. He was in his middle twenties, short, stocky, powerful and quite handsome with his face half in shadow, half in the faintly pink light of the rising sun. He wore the standard uniform of his rank and specialty . . . light brown coveralls, dark brown leather boots and pocketbelt. His bronze insignia and fingerwatch glinted. His crew-cut hair was carrot red.

He glanced at his fingerwatch again. *What's keeping them?*

Nervously, he began drumming on the tabletop with his fingertips.

The panel in the sky slid open again and Chief Engineer Dutton stepped through, saluting smartly. Phillips responded with a nod, not bothering to stand. Commodore Briggs, the great Commodore Abraham Briggs, would not have approved of a perfunctory salute like that, but Briggs was not there. Briggs was dead. Dutton realized this, understood the meaning of every gesture and lack of gesture and said nothing. Thin, gray-haired old Dutton had known Briggs since officers' training at New Annapolis on Luna. Like Briggs, he was a spit-and-polish man, a tight-ship man, a by-the-book man, and very, very careful. Phillips didn't like him.

"Have a seat."

The older man sat down at the far end of the table.

"They got Briggs," sighed Phillips.

"I haven't seen the body."

"Don't get any false hopes up, Dutton. There's not one chance in a million—"

"The commodore is a hard man to kill, sir."

"You don't have to do that."

"Do what, sir?"

"Call me sir. My name is Mike. You don't have to call me sir."

"I'd prefer it, sir."

Mike sat back with a sigh. "Things are going to be

different around here now. You might as well get used to
—it. I'm not like Briggs, you know."

"I know, sir." Dutton's carefully correct voice contained
a faint trace of irony.

The panel in the sky opened again to admit a dark
young man—black hair and an olive skin—wearing the
red coveralls of damage control. He, too, saluted smartly,
his heels coming together with an audible click.

"Ensign Peter DeCarli reporting, sir!"

"At ease, DeCarli," said Mike. "How's it going?"

"I have a team cutting into the main control room
now, sir," answered DeCarli.

"Any sign of life?" asked Dutton, trying to sound
casual.

"Nothing," said DeCarli, but when he saw the expression on Dutton's face he added hastily, "Of course it's
too early to know for sure."

"Where's Ensign Christina Enge?" demanded Mike. "I
want all the remaining officers here. We need someone to
represent the ship's medical staff, and she's in charge of
that now."

"If her superior officer is among those dead," put in
Dutton. There was a heavy silence.

"Miss Enge is with the damage control unit," said De-
Carli. "She wants to supervise the medical side of the . . .
rescue herself. She had . . . I mean she has a kind of
special feeling for the old commodore."

Mike frowned. "She could have sent a substitute."

"She's rather upset, sir," replied DeCarli nervously.

"Never mind, never mind," said Mike with a vague
gesture. "Be seated, DeCarli."

DeCarli took the seat next to Dutton. Mike had a feeling they were trying to keep as far away from him as
possible. Resentment was silent but real, as if Mike had
killed the commodore himself, as if Mike were some kind
of mutineer.

The panel opened again, and a group of men and
women entered and saluted. The blue coveralls of the

police, the brown for soldier, the black for clergy, the green for hydroponic aquaculturist.

"Isn't there anyone here from navigation?" Mike could not conceal his dismay.

The little group glanced at each other, then Ensign Reverend Richard Ellington stepped forward and said, "I'm afraid not, sir. They were all attending a briefing session in the main control room at the time of the attack."

"All of them?" asked Mike incredulously. "Not even one tiny little goldbricker in sick bay?"

Ellington shook his head. "You know the commodore didn't allow goldbricking." Dutton looked up sharply, and Mike gathered it was because Reverend Ellington had spoken about the commodore in the past tense.

"I see," said Mike softly, then gestured for them all to be seated. For a moment the squeak of chairs drowned out the muffled sound of the surf and the cries of the gulls. Mike poured himself a glass of water and drank deeply.

He began, "I know things seem bad, but they're not hopeless. The computer is down, but it can be repaired. How long would you say, DeCarli?"

DeCarli's brow furrowed thoughtfully. "Between a month and three weeks."

"That's too long."

DeCarli answered with a silent shrug.

"Can't you do it in two weeks, with help from other departments?"

DeCarli shook his head. "Other people would only be in the way. With other people helping, it could take years. Three weeks is the very best we can hope for."

"Sir," broke in Dutton.

"Yes, Dutton?"

"We don't have three weeks." The old chief engineer appeared even more pale and gray than usual, more gaunt and skeletal.

"Why not?"

"That burst of near light velocity, sir. It takes energy to

maintain inertialess drive at those speeds. It takes energy to accelerate and more energy to decelerate, to maintain the stasis field against the increase in mass—"

"What are you driving at, Dutton?" demanded Mike, although he already knew what Dutton was about to say. It wasn't hard to guess.

"We're low on energy, sir."

"How low?"

"If we're careful, sir, we can last a week, then we're finished. No drive, no computer. . . ."

"And no life support," added a woman in green coveralls. There was a murmur of apprehension.

Mike raised his hand for silence. "Is there someone here from instruments?"

"Here, sir," came an uncertain voice.

"Are there any stars within range where we could make a stellar tap and refill our energy banks?"

"One, sir, but—"

"No buts!" snapped Mike, half-rising.

"Sir," the voice continued. It was Walter Hughes, a genius with instruments of all kinds. "A stellar tap is always dangerous. It could cause certain imbalances in the star's core. It could trigger a supernova."

"So? We can make the tap and if the damn star blows, it blows. Supernovas happen all the time. We'll be far enough away so it won't get us. Is that all?"

"No, I'm sorry, sir, but that's not all." Hughes was looking down, not meeting Mike's eyes.

"Spit it out, Hughes," growled Mike.

"According to our readings, some form of intelligent life exists on the second planet of this stellar system. The other planets are gaseous. If the star blows, that's the end of all life on that planet. We've picked up fragmentary radio messages, sir. We're too far away to make any sense out of them, but they are definitely the product of some fairly advanced civilization."

Mike settled back in his chair with a grunt. "Maybe

there won't be any supernova. Some stars can take a tap and some can't. Maybe this is one of the stable ones."

"Maybe," said Dutton gloomily. "Maybe not. We've no way of telling without a computer—a master computer. There's too much relevant data to coordinate."

"So we're back to the computer again," sighed Mike.

Dutton answered, "That's right, sir."

"No chance of reaching some other stellar system?" Mike asked him.

"None whatever," Dutton replied, then added, "Sir."

"Not enough energy left," put in DeCarli.

Mike glared around the table, his eyes moving slowly from one to another of his fellow crewmen. "If I didn't know better, I'd say you were all involved in a plot against my life."

There was a flurry of nervous laughter. Dutton pointed out quietly, "We're on this ship too, sir."

After a long silence, Mike said slowly, "Check . . . and mate."

Dutton leaned forward. "There's one of us who hasn't been heard from yet, sir."

"Oh?" said Mike, a faint note of hope in his voice.

"The commodore," said Dutton.

"The commodore is dead, Dutton," Mike said with suppressed anger.

"We don't really know that, sir," insisted Dutton.

"I could call damage control," suggested DeCarli with false cheerfulness.

"Do that little thing," said Mike, barely audible.

"Christina?" DeCarli called out.

Instantly a voice answered from the sky. "Christina here. I'm sorry I didn't call before. We've been so busy. We found the commodore."

"And he's dead?" demanded Mike with an air of finality.

"No, no, he's not! He's hurt, unconscious, yes, but he's still breathing. Thank God he's still breathing!"

CHAPTER 2

Two hours later the *Corregidor* settled into a parking
ellipse, orbiting the planet from which they had received
the faint radio transmissions. Along its vast length, hull
lights began to wink out; in order to conserve energy,
Mike had ordered all the sections not essential to life
support closed down. The stasis field was the first to be
turned off. Now there would be no artificial gravity, let
alone right-angle turns at thousands of kilometers an hour
or instant reverses of direction. Certainly there would be
no accelerations to near light speed. Next the ionic drive
itself was shut off. A stable orbit didn't require it. The
ship could, with no additional expenditure of energy, continue to drift like an artificial moon around this planet
for the next two or three billion years.

The weapons rooms were the next to blink off. There
seemed no need for defence against the planet below. The
natives showed no sign of hostility; in fact, no sign that
they were even aware of the *Corregidor*'s presence.

The lights were killed in the rear storage areas, the
factory complexes and large portions of the crew's quarters.
Like a city, just before dawn, the lights flickered out, one
after the other; and night lifted as the starship drifted out
of the planet's shadow and glistened—a fantastic, white
stalactite in the sunlight.

In the complex of windows near the ugly, blackened
gash on the forward section the lights remained dim, as
they did in the secondary control room and in the region
of the hydroponic gardens and life-support system. Nothing that was not absolutely necessary could be allowed to
remain on. That was Mike's order.

The holovision mirage in the conference room was not
essential. When Mike once again gathered his officers together, they viewed the naked off-white plastic walls that

before had seemed like mountains, seascapes, forests, parks or the halls of famous buildings. In the dim, slightly yellow light the walls looked cheap, tawdry. Mike had a distinct feeling of claustrophobia. The room had always been small of course, but he had never before realized how small.

Also, gravity was absent.

It was hard to get used to the magnetic boots, hard to always remember that if you didn't walk slowly and carefully, you might find yourself drifting upward to bump gently against the ceiling. When Mike seated himself at the head of the table, he took the precaution of belting himself down, using an ordinary uniform belt as a makeshift safety belt. The others, as they filed in, did the same.

Mike began, "I've called you here again to—"

Chief Engineer Dutton interrupted, "Sir?"

Something in Dutton's voice put Mike on his guard. The old geezer was up to something! All the same Mike let him speak. "What is it, Dutton?"

"I don't want to seem to be insubordinate but. . . ." The gaunt old man glanced around at the others as if for moral support. *Oh oh*, thought Mike, *here it comes.*

Dutton licked his lips and continued. "I have to question the wisdom of turning off the weapons complexes. I realize it requires a certain amount of energy to keep them at the ready, but—"

"Are you worried about the natives?" Mike broke in.

"Yes, sir, but not only the natives. If they are still using ordinary radio for surface-to-surface communication, they are probably too backward to be able to attack us up here. It's the Lorns I'm thinking of, sir."

"The Lorns? What Lorns? There aren't any Lorns within light-years of here, unless you've been keeping something from me." Mike stared at the old man with open suspicion until he noticed that some of the others were looking at him with equal suspicion. *They think I'm getting paranoid.* He was appalled.

"I'd better explain, sir," said Dutton carefully. "You thought you succeeded in evading those two ships that attacked us——"

"What do you mean 'thought'?"

"They can track us, sir. We've left a trail. At near light speeds we develop quite a lot of mass, as you know. The free hydrogen in the space we've passed through will be disturbed . . . we'll have left a kind of wake behind us, invisible to the naked eye but not to the proper instruments."

Mike felt suddenly ill. The old man was right, of course. "While you're questioning things," said Mike, "why don't you question the rest of the decisions I've made since taking over command? Let's have everything out in the open!"

Dutton said softly, "Very well, sir. I'll be as brief as possible. I hope you realize that it is as painful to me as it is to you——"

"Spit it out, Dutton," growled Mike.

"Commodore Briggs, sir, would not have run away. He would have stood and fought." Dutton's voice was emotionless as a computer's, but Mike knew that behind that impassive facade, the chief engineer was boiling. Was it dislike or contempt?

"Even two to one?" asked Mike. "Even with no computer? Even with the commanding officer dead?"

"You were the commanding officer, sir." Now the contempt was no longer concealed.

"Whether you like it or not," said Mike softly, "I saved your life. I saved all our lives."

"For a few days, perhaps, sir. But the Lorns will arrive here and find us with our energy banks empty, our weapons shut down. Before, we had a chance. Now. . . ." Dutton threw up his hands in a gesture of despair, almost apathy.

DeCarli put in, "The Lorns don't take prisoners. You see? There's a bright side to every situation." He grinned at his own gallows humor, before adding more soberly, "But I think their intelligence service would love to collect the *Corregidor* as a souvenir. There's nothing they'd find more educational."

"It would be the first time they've ever been able to examine one of our ships-of-the-line all in one piece," said Dutton. Implied but unspoken was the idea that.all the others had fought until they were either victorious or blown to bits. Human science was in advance of Lorn science in some small but important ways. If the Lorns had a chance to examine the *Corregidor* intact, that advantage would vanish.

"You've worked this all out among yourselves, haven't you?" said Mike. "You've made up your minds . . . behind my back."

Dutton said, "You've always been such a democratic officer, sir. You've often said that the decisions of the captain should be put to a vote, not only by the junior officers, but by the whole crew. Certainly you can't object if we—"

"Come to the point, Dutton," said Mike. It wasn't paranoia. They really had made up their minds behind his back. They were looking at each other now as if they'd won some kind of victory . . . but what kind of victory was possible under the circumstances? It was obvious that they wanted to blow up the ship, that the crew of the *Corregidor* was going to "succeed" in doing something the Lorns had been trying to do since the war began. That was the "victory" they had in mind. Mike could either agree and join them, or disagree and be outvoted by them. It wasn't much of a choice.

"That's an Earth-type planet down there," continued Dutton with a vague gesture.

"We'll all shuttle down and live happily ever after," finished Mike mockingly.

The chief engineer reddened. "Something like that, sir."

"Then we blow the *Corregidor* to atoms. Right?" Mike made no attempt to hide his bitterness.

"While we still have the energy in our banks to do it," added Dutton. The old man's self-control slipped a little; his voice shook as he spoke and his eyes were glittering with moisture. Mike realized it hadn't been an easy decision for Dutton to make.

For a moment Mike felt like trying to do something, anything, to stop them, then realized the futility of his position. "Take a vote on it," he murmured, staring at his hands.

He had spoken so softly Dutton hadn't understood. The old man leaned forward and asked, "What's that?"

"Vote! Go ahead and vote!" Mike shouted, glaring around.

The hands were already going up, even though the motion had not yet been properly stated. "Those in favor," called out Dutton. He looked around, counting.

"Those opposed?" No hands were raised.

Mike had abstained.

The tears in Dutton's eyes looked fake because he somehow managed to keep his usual military poker face, in spite of everything. "That's it," he said hoarsely. It was the most disorganized and improper process of decision-making Mike had ever seen on the *Corregidor*. Commodore Briggs, he reflected with irony, would never have allowed it.

Mike was looking down, unbuckling the belt that held him to his chair, when he heard a familiar voice roar out, "I veto that proposal!"

Mike raised his head and stared at the entrance panel and at the man who stood in the doorway, pale, disheveled, and slightly swaying.

It was Commodore Abraham Briggs.

"You're here," said Dutton stupidly. "How . . . ?"

"I held my breath, Mister Dutton," grunted the commodore, sliding a magnetized chair up to the table and sitting in it. Christina was about to help him strap himself down —she knew that he must be in considerable pain—but he seemed to manage all right by himself.

A long, uncomfortable silence ensued as the commodore's gaze moved from one face to another in the group.

"So," said Briggs at last, "you've voted to blow up my ship. There're few enough starships as it is! The *Corregidor* can't be spared."

Dutton began, "Allow me to explain, sir."

Briggs glared at him and the old man almost lost his voice.

"I'm waiting," prompted the commodore.

"The computer's out," said Dutton. "We can't fix it before the energy runs out."

"That's right, sir," put in DeCarli quickly.

"So we can't compute our position," said Dutton. "We can't tell one star from another."

"The devil you say!" snorted Briggs. "I take it you've never heard of the spectrograph! Every star has its own spectrographic pattern, as individual to that star as a fingerprint is to a man."

"But all that information is in the computer," said Dutton miserably.

"Not all of it, thank God," growled Briggs. "There's a little of it here, too." He tapped his balding head with a stubby, powerful finger. He was a man of imposing appearance at any time; close to two meters in height, 50 years old or thereabouts, with an athletic build and a military bearing, glittering black eyes and bushy iron-gray eyebrows, a broad protuberant nose and heavy jaw, and a thick, bull neck like a wrestler's . . . he sometimes reminded Christina of a huge shambling bear. Now he looked more imposing than ever, perhaps because the organic bandage above his left eye had not yet grown and blended in with his natural skin. It made him look like a troll, or perhaps a sullen gladiator.

"Even you," said Dutton, somewhat awed, "can't have memorized the spectrographic pattern of every star in the galaxy."

"Of course not," growled Briggs. "I'm not omnipotent, Mister Dutton, though you may have heard rumors to the contrary. If I can identify just three stars out of the thousands that are doubtless visible from here, that will be quite enough for a rough triangulation of our position. You mean you were going to blow up my ship just because—"

"There's also the matter of the Lorns," said Dutton. "The Lorns, sir."

"What Lorns?"

"The Lorns who attacked us. The Lorns who almost killed you. They might follow us here . . . we've left a trail through space a child could follow."

"Indeed? And what if they don't follow us? What, Mister Dutton, if they have better things to do? Are we going to do their job for them?"

"No, sir," said Dutton lamely. "But if the *Corregidor* falls into enemy hands. . . ."

"Then, sir, will be the time to blow her up," said Briggs triumphantly. "Before that, sir, it is our duty to fight for her to the last man."

Mike said, "They were going to abandon ship, sir. They were going to shuttle down to the planet we're circling now—"

"Did you think you'd be safe there?" thundered Briggs to the cowering officers. "The Lorns would wipe you out and every other living thing on that planet! You know they allow no life they don't create themselves! If we've brought the Lorns to this planet, we owe it to the inhabitants to defend them, whoever they might be." Briggs paused, pursing his lips, and demanded coldly, "Who ordered the weapons turned off?"

At last Dutton had a chance to shift the blame. He pointed a shaking finger at Mike and exclaimed, "Lieutenant Phillips, sir!"

"I'm not surprised," said Briggs, turning to Mike. "Well, Mister Phillips, we'll just have to turn them back on again, won't we?"

DeCarli broke in, "We have to turn off something. The energy—"

"Turn off the hospital!" snapped Briggs.

Christina had been standing behind Briggs, amused, her long hair, blond streaked with gray, drifting in the zero-gravity as if she were under water. Now her smile vanished. "What?"

The commodore wrenched himself around in his chair to stare her down. "Woman!" he rumbled. "We won't need it unless we lose, and then, I'm sure, the Lorns won't give us time to use it."

She started to speak, but saw from the commodore's face she would be wasting her breath.

"Secondary bridge!" called out Phillips, activating the intercom with these key words.

"Bridge here," came a voice from the ceiling.

Mike relayed the order to activate the weapons system and deactivate the hospital complex. "Aye, sir," answered the secondary bridge. Then he added, "We're picking up those radio signals from the planet again, sir. It's very strange."

"Strange?" said Briggs, eyebrows rising.

"Commodore? Is that you? Yes, sir. The natives, whoever they are, are speaking English. They have a foreign accent that makes it a little hard to understand them, but it's undoubtedly English."

The officers looked at each other in surprise.

Briggs said, "It must be one of our colonies! I hope all you idiots realize what this means. You almost blew up the *Corregidor* for nothing! Now all we have to do to get out of our present predicament is shuttle down to the planet's surface and find a bit of help. They can tell us where we are, lend us a computer to calculate if a stellar tap is possible, and if it isn't, tell us which way to beam our sos. If we're orbiting an Earth colony, we can't be too far from human-occupied territory."

Still worried, Dutton objected, "Something's wrong, sir, English or no English. Why no gravatic wave transmissions? Or even television? Why no welcoming party or any attempt to contact us by radio? They must know we're here."

"Are you sure they must know we're here?" demanded Briggs.

"Unless they lack, not only radar, but simple telescopes," said Dutton.

Briggs mused a while, forehead furrowed, iron-gray brows meeting in a puzzled frown. After a moment, thoughtfully stroking his chin with his fingertip, he murmured, "I see what you mean." Then, slapping his palm on the table, he made his decision. "We'll have to go down and have a look! That's all there is to it!"

"As your doctor, I'd advise. . . ." began Christina, leaning forward, but the commodore silenced her with an impatient gesture.

"Leave me alone, woman! First contacts can be touchy. Do you for one moment think I trust any of these imbeciles to do the job?" He roared at the ceiling, "Make ready the *Manta!*" The *Manta* was the shuttlecraft, and it really did resemble a giant manta ray, streamlined for entry and flight in planetary atmospheres. He turned to his crew and continued, "I'm leaving Dutton in charge here. I want Mister Phillips with me, where he can't do any more damage."

Mike winced.

Dutton answered briskly, "Aye, sir!"

"And as for the rest of you lunatics," continued Briggs, his eyes moving from one face to another, "I want you to try to resist the temptation to blow up the ship until I return. Only if you are actually about to be taken by the enemy are you to even dream of destroying the *Corregidor*. Is that understood?"

"Aye, sir," came a feeble chorus of voices.

"Doctor Enge!" Briggs called Christina "Doctor" as a mark of respect when he was feeling particularly well disposed toward her. "When you saved my life . . ." he hesitated, embarrassed, "did you also save my . . . ahem . . . claymore?"

"Aye, sir," she returned, smiling indulgently. She was thinking how childish the commodore was about certain things. The claymore was his favorite toy . . . more than a toy, his symbol of identity, like the western pearl-handled revolvers of the twentieth-century general, Patton. It was a sword, an antique, Scottish ceremonial sword he wore mainly on diplomatic missions. Fencing was the commodore's way of keeping fit on long voyages, and he was an expert swordsman. Christina turned and headed for the door, walking with that odd, careful shuffle dictated by lack of gravity conditions. With magnetic boots, one should never have both feet off the floor at once.

"Meet me at the shuttle-bay, doctor," Briggs called after her. He turned again to his officers and barked, "Dismissed!"

A low murmur of voices broke out, together with the sound of chairs, on magnetic castors, being slid back from the table. Briggs shambled toward the door, gesturing at Phillips to follow.

When he came close, Phillips saw beads of sweat on the commodore's forehead and a certain tightness around his eyes.

"Are you feeling all right, sir?" asked Mike in a low voice.

Briggs nodded without speaking, but Mike was fairly sure his commanding officer was lying. The commodore was not quite recovered from his narrow escape but clearly would not allow this to stop him from carrying out his duties. Briggs had always been like that. To him sickness or any other kind of physical weakness was like an insult to his personal honor. Also, Mike thought, the commodore was more worried than he dared admit in front of the others.

"BEFORE putting one's head in a lion's mouth," said Abraham Briggs, "it is wise to get a report on his teeth."

"Aye, sir," agreed Mike, following the commodore into the instrument room.

Morgan, in the gray coveralls of instrumentman, looked up, slightly startled, jerked off his earphones and, finding himself strapped down, saluted as best he could from a sitting position.

"At ease, Mister Morgan," said Briggs gruffly. "Anything new on the situation planetside?"

"Not much," admitted Morgan, checking over the notes on his clipboard. "There seems to be a network of small radio stations—they might be nothing more powerful than walkie-talkies—and one big base station. The walkie-talkies don't move, but the big base station does. All the time we've been monitoring it, it's been progressing slowly but steadily across the planet's face, never going more than about 40 kilometers per hour. None of the stations is on the air continuously. Each just snaps on, says a few words, then snaps off, and in between there's not even a carrier wave."

"Hmm. I see," muttered Briggs, frowning. "But when they do talk, what do they say?"

"Well, it's all in English, but some kind of in-group jargon. With the computer we might . . . but that's out of the question." A light appeared, a wavering red, on the instrument panel. "There's one now," said Morgan hopefully. "Want to listen in?"

"Let's hear it," commanded Briggs.

Morgan gestured over a stud and a crisp, businesslike voice sounded through the loudspeaker. "Zone seven, Ecolog," it said. "We see you. Copesetic. Out!"

It had been a man's voice, a deep bass. Now came a

woman's voice, stronger and clearer. "Continue norm, zone seven. Out!"

Abruptly there was nothing but the hiss and crackle of random static.

"Interesting," said Briggs.

"But not very helpful," added Mike.

"I wouldn't say that, Mister Phillips. That word 'cope-setic' is obsolete military slang. It comes, if I recall correctly, from a Creole French expression meaning 'able to be coped with.' "

"So?"

"So, Mister Phillips, it would seem that our friends down there were once a part of the Earth empire, but have been separated from it for a long time. It is often the case that isolated societies preserve certain linguistic peculiarities long after they have gone out of style in the mainstream culture. Take the case of the English preserved in the backwaters of American Appalachia—"

"The woman's voice came from the moving base station," put in Morgan. "The man's voice came from the walkie-talkie—if it is a walkie-talkie. They're all broadcasting on the same wavelength."

"Ah yes," murmured Briggs. "Didn't you notice something about that woman's voice? A certain pride, a certain arrogance even? That woman, whoever she is, is in the habit of being obeyed . . . obeyed instantly, without question. That other word . . . Ecolog. That would seem to be derived from another obsolete expression, 'ecology,' a term used in the late twentieth and early twenty-first century to denote the study of an environment and all the life forms contained in it. What, then, would an Ecolog be? Perhaps someone who studies an environment and all the life forms it contains . . . perhaps more than that. It could mean someone who *controls* an environment and all the life forms in it!"

"Let's take a look at the surface," said Mike, moving

toward the videotelescope. "That should give us something a little more solid to go on."

"First," said Briggs, "allow me to venture, sir, a prediction. Prediction is, of course, the very soul of science! I predict that we shall find a planet whose inhabitants appear, in spite of their anachronistic use of radio, to be living at a technological level no higher than Earth's Dark Ages."

The techman at the controls of the videotelescope was amazed. "Why that's exactly right, Commodore! How did you guess?"

Briggs was pleased. "I do not guess, mister. Let's have a look." He peered into the picture tube, thoughtfully chewing on his fingertip. "Yes. Yes. The pattern is becoming quite clear now."

Looking over the commodore's shoulder, Mike had a bird's-eye view of a walled city in a desert. Judging from the long shadows, it was dawn down there. Briggs gestured over the studs and the scene shifted. A forest, a river, mountains, a road along which a caravan was slowly making its way came into view. The animals loaded with cargo were alien—some sort of eight-legged monsters—but otherwise Mike could have been looking down on Earth as it had been in the first century AD. And there was no doubt that the beings they could see were humans. Briggs increased the amplification, and they saw one fellow, bearded and wearing a dirty yellow robe, so clearly they could make out the brownish color of his eyes.

"Obscene!" grunted Briggs.

"What?" said Mike.

"I was reading the lips of that man down there. He speaks English all right, but not the English of a gentleman!"

The techman broke in, "I'd like to show you something, sir, while you're here. We've been scratching our heads over it for hours." He was adjusting the direction of the videotelescope with a few expert gestures over the studs. "Where did that thing go? Ah, there it is!"

At first glance Mike thought it was a spacecraft, though it was slowly drifting about 300 meters high in the air; it was a long, slender, cigar-shaped vessel.

"Must be supported by some sort of anti-gravity device," commented Mike.

Briggs laughed outright. "Nonsense, my boy! Don't you know what that thing is? Why, it's a dirigible, of course!"

CHAPTER 3

"The claymore, Doctor Enge," commanded Abraham Briggs.

She handed him his sword, and he gravely strapped it on.

"If I could go with you—" she began.

"Out of the question," he snorted. As if ashamed of being so short with her, he reached out and took her hand, adding softly, "You understand, of course."

She sighed and nodded.

He turned and clambered over the wing and through the air lock into the *Manta* where Mike, at the shuttle-craft's controls, sat waiting for him. The outer air-lock door swung shut and sealed itself, followed by the inner air-lock door. The commodore glanced around at the eight-man squad of brown-coveralled soldiers strapped down in the narrow passenger compartment. Satisfied, he took his place beside Mike in the copilot's seat.

"*Manta One* requesting takeoff clearance," said Mike into his helmet microphone.

"On the count of three," came the controller's voice in his earphones. "One, two, three."

The panels in the *Corregidor*'s wall opened so swiftly that the rush of escaping air, combined with the push supplied by the reverse of polarity in the magnetic clamps, carried the *Manta* out into the void without any use of its own power.

As the sliding doors quickly slid shut behind them and the *Manta* continued to drift away from the mother ship, Mike got his first look at the planet with his naked eye. The useful but somewhat distorting videotelescope remained on board the mother ship.

"Why," he said with awe, "it looks just like Earth! What a strange coincidence!"

"Don't ask too much of coincidence, Mister Phillips. No, this planet is the way it is because someone made it that way."

"God?" Mike half joked.

"No, but perhaps someone regarded as a god by the present inhabitants."

The voice of the controller crackled over the earphones. "We're broadcasting power to you now, sir. You can start your engines any time."

"Thank you," answered Briggs crisply. "Let's go."

Mike gestured over the studs on his control panel and the force of acceleration pressed them gently back into their seats as the engines came to life with a rising whine of energy. The *Corregidor* was behind them now, invisible through the ports but still to be seen on the small monitor screen in the center of the instrument panel, a steadily dwindling black and white image.

"Controller," said Briggs. "Where's that dirigible now?"

There was a moment's pause before the answer, "It must be on the other side of the planet, sir. At any rate we seem to have lost track of it."

Another voice broke in . . . Christina Enge. "Briggs?" She sounded worried.

"Yes?" said the commodore.

After a long pause, Christina sighed, "Nothing."

The controller came on again. "Good luck, sir."

"Thank you," said Abraham Briggs.

There was no further communication from the *Corregidor*. Briggs switched over from gravatic wave to radio and tuned to the frequency the natives had been using. For a while there was nothing but white noise; then suddenly a carrier wave came on and a male voice said, "Zone twenty-four. We see you. Can you pick up cargo? Over."

The woman's voice again, proud and commanding, "Affirmative. Stand by at the mooring mast. Out."

The carrier wave vanished and the white noise returned.

Mike examined his instruments and said quietly, "We

hit the upper atmosphere in—let's see—exactly 12 minutes and 15 seconds."

Briggs nodded, chewing on the tip of his index finger; it was obvious his mind was on other things.

LIKE a vulture the *Manta* glided downward in lazy circles. The engines were off and the only sound was the rush of air along the shuttlecraft's outer surfaces. A moment before, the atmosphere had been heating the little ship to a red glow, but now that they had slowed, the wind was having a cooling effect.

"There's a city," said Mike, pointing.

"I see," said Briggs. "Let's land as close as we can to it."

From the shadows below they estimated that it was early in the morning.

"We might upset the natives, coming down from the sky like this in an alien flying machine," said Mike.

"No doubt we will, Mister Phillips," agreed the commodore, "but it can't be helped."

They swept in low over the rooftops, banking steeply, watching for some sign of hostility. All was quiet. They climbed once again into the yellowish gray light of dawn, then made another low-level pass over the city. Still no sign of danger. Mike and Briggs looked at each other and Briggs nodded, smiling, but Mike saw that he was pale and tense. Mike brought the streamlined, white *Manta* to a standstill in the air about 30 meters above a spot some distance from what seemed to be the main gate of the city.

"Still no sign of anybody." Mike was somewhat relieved. "I guess they're keeping out of sight."

"Can you blame them?"

They both laughed nervously. All around them, as far as the eye could see, lay desert, without a trace of man or animal. "Set 'er down," commanded Briggs softly.

Gently, carefully, the little flying wing settled toward

the ridge of a dune until, with a soft bump and a rasp of sand against metal, it was down. The whine of the engines died away to a dull hum, a trickle of power "just in case."

Mike gazed at his instruments in surprise. "The air is Earth-normal, sir. Exactly Earth-normal."

"As I expected."

"And the virus and bacteria counts are below Earth-normal. In fact, there don't seem to be any microbiological forms that might be hostile to us." Mike was more surprised still.

"Paradise, mister. In a way it seems a shame to disturb it."

"We're germ-free ourselves, commodore."

"I wasn't thinking of germs, Phillips. It's what's in our minds that's a danger. We may bring this whole civilization down like a precarious house of cards." He began unstrapping himself, adding fatalistically, "So be it."

The man's voice on the radio suddenly announced, "Aliens down. Over."

The woman's voice answered, with an unmistakable undertone of triumph, "Thank you."

An instant later the hum of engines died and every light in the *Manta* went out.

"It's impossible to jam a power transmission," insisted Mike.

"Impossible for us, perhaps," answered Briggs, taking a handkerchief from his spun steel pocketbelt and wiping his forehead. The sun was as yet low in the sky, but already the desert was heating up.

"For us? I thought you said we were in advance of the people on this planet!"

"I was wrong, incredible as that may seem. It would appear we are dealing, not with some backward medieval intelligence, but with a seventh level mind—at least seventh level—that delights in temporal eclecticism. A little something from the Middle Ages, a little something from the first century AD, a charming dirigible from the 1930s and, for spice, a dash of the distant future!" Mike was appalled, but his commanding officer seemed to take a perverse pleasure in the seriousness of their situation.

With a crank they had managed to open manually an emergency exit atop the fuselage and now squatted on the dune near the crippled white *Manta*. Their eight-man squad of soldiers crouched in a rough circle around them, weapons ready to hold off any possible attackers, though there was still not a soul in sight.

"What now?" Mike would almost have welcomed the sight of an enemy at this moment. At least then he would have been able to do something.

"Calm yourself, Lieutenant," said Briggs sharply. "Remember, if you can, that you are a soldier. Our mission is to contact the natives of this planet and seek their help. Correct? Then that is what we'll do. Nothing has changed, really, except that we have more reason to hope that our hosts will have a computer advanced enough for our needs."

The commodore turned toward a trio of soldiers cowering in the shuttle's shadow—they seemed, if anything, to be the most frightened in the whole troop—and called out, "You there! You three. Come with us. The rest of you stay here and guard the *Manta*."

The three stepped forward somewhat reluctantly.

"And you over there," continued Briggs, his eye fixing on another "volunteer." "I want you to write a message in the sand. Yes you! Nice big letters now, so the *Corregidor* can see them with the videotelescope on their next pass overhead. Tell them—let's see—tell them 'Power out. Continuing mission. Await orders.' Hmm. Yes. That about covers it. I hope it will keep those fools up there from sending down another shuttle to join us . . . in this trap."

"Aye, sir," said the soldier uncertainly. He began marking out the message in the sand, scuffing along with his boots.

"Who's the senior officer in the squad?" demanded Briggs.

"Me, sir . . . I think." A short, intellectual-looking fellow with thick glasses held up his hand. Briggs gazed at him a moment, then sighed and said, "Very well, sir. You'll be in charge. If we don't return by sundown, come after us. We may need rescuing. Otherwise wait for further orders. Is that understood?"

"Yes, sir!" A snappy salute.

Briggs smiled. Mike knew the commodore was always impressed by a show of discipline. As long as the salutes were right, everything was right as far as old Briggs was concerned!

"You, Phillips, and you three soldiers come with me. Cheer up, gentlemen. We're only going for a little walk into town. Who knows? There may be beautiful young ladies waiting there to be liberated. That would suit you lecherous swine, I'm sure. Now, forward march! Hup two three four!"

They set off in a straggling line toward the gate of the walled city, and the hot wind picked up the dust from their footprints and whirled it aloft in a swirling yellow cloud. The gate was wide open. If these were hostile natives, why didn't they close the gate? Why didn't they man the walls and start shooting?

As they neared the entrance Briggs became more cautious. "Fan out," he ordered, with a gesture. "Move in quickly now, but don't shoot unless someone shoots at you."

"Aye, sir," came the replies as the little party split up and began moving in toward the gate, crouching and half-running.

A moment later they were through the gateway. Briggs straightened up and, shielding his eyes from the sun with his hand, turned slowly around. There were the buildings . . . military buildings, stables, two-story living quarters of rough baked clay, even an inn, marked by a faded sign with a picture of a mug of beer on it. The sign swung in the breeze with a creaking sound that was almost the only relief from the oppressive silence.

"Nobody home," whispered one of the soldiers.

"A ghost town," said another with awe.

"So it would appear," snapped Abraham Briggs. "Search it!"

MIKE stepped out of the darkened doorway into the ruddy glow of the setting sun. Briggs, seated on the edge of a well in the center of the city square, stopped fanning himself with his helmet long enough to call out, "Hey there, Lieutenant Phillips! Found anything?"

Wearily Mike shuffled through the dust toward the well, holding up a can. "Another plastic can, sir," he answered with disgust.

"But this one, unless my eyes deceive me, is unopened."

Mike seated himself beside Briggs and handed him the can, and the commodore examined it with some interest. Mike wondered what sense Briggs could be making out of it. One more can! They had found so many plastic cans and bottles today, most of them empty. They had found furniture, too, and ancient rotting clothing, but no people . . . not even any human bones. "And the label, as usual, is in English, whatever that may mean."

Briggs read the words, "peanut butter." He looked up from the can and said, "Nothing is meaningless. It's just that we see, not with our eyes, but with our minds. The man with an untrained mind might as well be blind." He set the can down and began fanning himself again with his helmet.

"It'll be dark soon," said Mike, after a pause.

"I know."

"We'd better be heading back. No use getting everybody all upset."

The commodore stood up. "You're right, of course. Perfectly right. It's only that I'd hoped. . . ." He put on his helmet with an air of resignation, leaving his sentence unfinished.

A voice called out, "Commodore Briggs!"

Briggs brightened. "Hello. Maybe this is it." He cupped his hands around his mouth and shouted, "What is it?"

The answer echoed through the wide empty street. "Footprints, sir. Fresh ones. Over here."

The commodore had already broken into a run, heading in the direction of the voice. He called, "Stay there, man. I'm coming." Mike followed, walking quickly but unable to bring himself to run.

When he caught up, he found the commodore kneeling in a dark, dusty alley, examining something with his flashlight. Nearby stood the three soldiers, and one of them seemed quite proud of himself. Briggs looked up. "They're fresh, Mister Phillips! I'll wager they're not more than a few hours old."

Mike leaned over, noticing that whoever had left the prints had been barefoot.

"Small feet, wouldn't you say?" Briggs went on excitedly. "A child, perhaps. But running. Notice the distance between the prints."

"Bare feet," said Mike. "That means a savage."

"Beware of snap judgments, my boy." Briggs stood up. "Well, let's go. He took two steps in the direction the footprints led. The soldiers looked at each other uneasily. "We're going to follow them, of course," added Briggs, turning on them with a sullen frown.

"It'll be dark in a minute," ventured one of the troops.

"The others will think. . . ." began another.

Indeed the sun had gone down by now, and the light at the zenith was fading fast. A breeze stirred. A cool breeze. Briggs stood silent a moment before saying, "Quite right. Quite right. The lieutenant here has already been kind enough to inform me of that fact."

There was a heavy silence.

The commodore gripped the hilt of his Scottish sword

and broke the silence with, "I'm staying." He spoke casually, without expression.

"Alone?" asked Mike.

"If need be. Someone will have to go back to the *Manta* and report to the others, but I intend to follow these tracks. Of course, if there are any volunteers. . . ."

Nobody moved for a second, then Mike stepped to his side. The three soldiers remained rooted to their places.

"Excellent," said the Commodore stiffly. "Those also serve who only turn and run. Very well, you three, move!"

The soldiers did not need to be told twice. Crouching, casting fearful glances at every doorway and window they passed, they set off at a trot for the city gates.

"So, it's just you and I, eh?" said Briggs with satisfaction. "Well, what do you think of that?" He gave Phillips a mocking wink.

"I think you're a damn fool, sir."

"Indeed?"

"A man as valuable as you has no right to place himself in danger on an unimportant—"

"Unimportant, you say? It is my continued existence that is, in these circumstances, unimportant. If we fail to get help from the natives of this bloody planet, I may withdraw my veto against blowing up the *Corregidor* . . . and if and when the Lorns trace us here, that will be the end of us all."

Briggs turned and, with the aid of his flashlight, began following the footprints. Mike, right behind him, held a rocketdart stinger pistol at the ready.

THERE was no moonlight—this planet was without a satellite—but a vast, oval spiral nebula filled the sky, casting a spectral blue glow over the irregular looming hulks of the buildings.

The blonde crouched.

Through a crack in a decaying door, she could see the flashlight far down the street, crossing and recrossing from one curb to the other, as she had crossed and re-crossed, ducking in and out of doorways and passageways. At times the wind shifted, and she could hear soft voices, men's voices. *Are they after me?*

She realized that they were following her footprints . . . but how could she stop leaving footprints? Dust was every-where. And here, inside a building, the dust was worse than it was out in the streets.

Perhaps up on the rooftops. . . .

She left the door and pitter-pattered up a flight of stone steps, down a cobweb-choked hallway, up another flight of steps. An instant later she was on the roof, carefully picking her way over the slippery tiles.

Below her the door creaked open. The men were entering the building! She heard their voices again, closer than before, but still could not make out what they said.

She reached the edge of the roof and stopped.

It was a long jump to the next roof, and there was a two-story drop to the cobblestone street.

Her glance snapped to the right, to the left. Trapped!

A chimney was nearby. It might be big enough to hide behind. She scampered to it, climbed behind it, hanging on tight to the rough, rocky surface. She slipped and almost fell over the roof edge, but caught herself in time.

"What was that?" came a voice from inside the building.

She held her breath.

"Our friend with the bare feet, I hope," came another, deeper voice. "On the roof, I believe, Mister Phillips."

There was the sound of boots on the stone steps.

Peeping around the corner of the chimney, she caught a glimpse of a helmeted head silhouetted against the nebula, then another. A flashlight snapped on, and as it swung her way, she shrank back out of sight.

"It may be a trap, commodore," said the first man.

"And then again, it may not. If we sneak about I doubt that we'll fool anyone but ourselves, and it gives a better impression if we walk right in. The more harmless and defenseless we seem, the better, wouldn't you say, Phillips?"

"Maybe, but—"

"Hold on! I thought I saw something move . . . over there behind the chimney." The strangers spoke with a funny accent, but she understood one thing clearly enough. In another instant they'd have her!

She sprang from her hiding place and scampered frantically over the tiles.

"There he goes, sir!"

"After him, Phillips!"

The gulf between this roof and the next was just as wide on the opposite end, but without giving herself time to think about the danger, she launched herself into space.

With a grunt she landed on the neighboring roof, caught her balance and kept running. A thump and a curse told her one of the men had jumped across behind her.

"Jump, Phillips, damn you! If I can make it, so can you."

"I don't know—"

"Go down the steps then. Try to head him off. I haven't time to argue."

She opened a trapdoor, bolted down a flight of stairs, tripped, fell, jumped up again and kept running. It was so dark! She knew these buildings well, but in the dark even she could make mistakes.

And now the boots were behind her again, drumming down the stairs. She went down another flight four steps at a time. She was on the ground floor now and about to burst out through the front door when she remembered the other man had been ordered to head her off. He might be waiting for her in the street. She turned and headed instead for a side window. As she pulled open the shutter, a rusty hinge squeaked. The steps behind her stopped for a moment, then came toward her even more quickly than before.

She clambered over the windowsill and found herself

in a narrow passage between the buildings. She hesitated, wondering which way to run.

A flashlight flickered inside the room behind her.

"I see him, Lieutenant! This way!"

A distant voice somewhere beyond one end of the passage answered, "Aye, sir!"

She ran toward the other end.

A moment later she was in the open street, pounding along with head down and cornsilk hair streaming behind her.

She glanced back over her shoulder. One of the men was still after her and gaining. If only she had some shoes . . . the stones hurt her feet. Once she'd had shoes, so long ago she could hardly remember.

She ducked into an alley, then stopped abruptly. It was dark here, so dark she had almost run into the wall at the dead end without seeing it. Now there really was no escape.

She bent down and picked up a rock, weighing it in her hand, as the running steps grew steadily louder.

CHAPTER 4

Commodore Briggs had been misled by the small footprints—certainly some barefoot child could not be a menace—and had entered the mouth of the alley without his usual caution. He was thus totally unprepared for the impact of the heavy rock.

The rim of his helmet cushioned some of the blow—otherwise he would have been a dead man—but the stone rebounded and struck his forehead hard enough to stun him and make him drop his flashlight. The light bounced with a clatter across the paving stones and came to rest, still shining, but pointed away from him toward the street. As he staggered backward, trying to keep his balance, his unseen attacker rushed furiously out of the gloom and butted him in the stomach.

With a grunt Briggs fell, but as he went down his gloved hand lashed out and closed on a slender ankle. The attacker fell on him with a low, animallike growl, and he felt fingernails claw at his cheeks, seeking his eyes. Briggs was dazed and dizzy, but managed somehow to fend off those eager talons. His opponent was not very strong, but quick, desperate and utterly ruthless. They struggled in near silence; both were panting hoarsely but neither cried out until Briggs heard running footsteps approaching and called, "Phillips! Over here!"

Mike appeared at the mouth of the alley, gun in hand, crouching and peering into the blackness.

Briggs shouted, "The flashlight, you fool! Get the flashlight!"

"Aye, sir." Mike lunged forward and snatched up the light, swinging it instantly in the direction of the fight.

"Not in my eyes, damn it!" shouted Briggs, temporarily blinded. "Hang on to this rascal, will you? Before he gets away from us!"

"I've got him, sir."

With a sigh of relief, Briggs released his grip on the ankle. There was a sound of ripping cloth, then a cry of astonishment from Mike. "He's a . . . a she!"

The lithe stranger was running again. Briggs could hear the slap of bare feet on paving stones, could dimly see Mike standing with some shredded rags in his hands, staring.

"Don't just stand there, Phillips!" bellowed the commodore, but Mike seemed paralyzed.

At the mouth of the alley Briggs glimpsed a flash of flesh, a young girl running in the nebula-light. She was sprinting for the opposite side of the street, long tangled hair streaming behind her.

Briggs drew his stinger pistol, aimed and pulled the trigger.

The only sound was a faint snick as the tiny self-propelled homing dart flew from the muzzle.

The girl sucked in her breath sharply, took a few awkward steps, then fell sprawling, face down on the roadway.

"Did you kill her?" demanded Mike, dismayed.

"Of course not. I used the barbiturate darts, not the poison ones." Briggs clambered to his feet and stood, swaying.

"There's blood on your forehead, sir," said Mike.

"Oh? You don't say." The commodore removed a glove, touched his forehead experimentally, examined the dark stain on his fingertip. "I'll be all right."

The two men walked over to the unconscious girl.

"Pick her up, Lieutenant," commanded Briggs.

"Me, sir?"

"Who else?"

Mike handed Briggs the flashlight, then stooped and picked her up in his arms.

"Let's take her to the *Manta*, Lieutenant." Briggs's voice was gentle.

"Yes, sir."

The Ecolog

THE soldier snapped awake.

From the direction of the city two figures were approaching on foot.

"Halt! Who goes there?" demanded the soldier, a faint quiver of fear in his voice.

"Briggs and Phillips," came the reply. The commodore's voice was unmistakable. But something was wrong. Phillips was in his underwear and carrying what appeared to be a corpse.

Briggs, as he came closer to the *Manta* and its guard, noticed the puzzlement on the soldier's face. "We found a native. A girl. She didn't have any clothes of her own, so Mike decided to lend her his."

Indeed, Mike was carrying a girl, her arms and legs dangling awkwardly, and she was dressed in Mike's tan coveralls—a few sizes too big for her.

When Mike spoke, his teeth were chattering. "May I please go inside and w-warm u-up, sir?" he asked.

"Set the girl down on this dune here," Briggs commanded.

Mike set her down very carefully, saying, "She's regaining consciousness, sir."

"So much the better, Mister Phillips, and now . . . dismissed!"

Thankfully, Mike hurried toward the shelter of the shuttlecraft while the commodore knelt beside the faintly stirring form of the stranger. The guard looked on with curiosity.

Briggs asked softly, "Who are you, young lady?"

The girl opened her eyes. "What? Where?"

"I see you speak English."

She did not reply, but looked around her with a puzzled expression. At last her gaze fell on the *Manta*.

"No!" she cried out in sudden terror.

"What's wrong?" Briggs asked soothingly. "That's only our flying machine."

She sat up abruptly. "It's evil!"

Briggs chuckled. "Not evil really. A bit unreliable perhaps but—"

"No! Evil! It brings death!"

"Not at all. Why, if anything happens to the mother ship, this machine can actually save life. It can act as a sort of lifeboat."

She shook her head vigorously, her long hair swirling. "No! Not life! Death!" She tried to rise to her feet, but Briggs grasped her by the shoulder.

He said, "Calm down, my dear. I shall do my best to act like a gentleman if you will try to act like a lady."

She caught sight of the dried blood on his forehead. "Oh, did I hurt you?"

"It didn't feel too bad at the time, but I must admit I'm getting a frightful headache now."

She was calmer, more concerned than frightened. "I'm sorry, but you should not have chased me. I do not like to hurt people. I never bother anyone who does not threaten to take me back."

"Back where?"

"You know where! You must know!" Her hysteria was returning.

"Hush now. I'm not going to harm you. I just want to get to know you. Allow me to introduce myself. I'm Commodore Abraham Briggs, commanding officer of the starship *Corregidor*."

She stared at him without comprehension.

"And now," he prompted, "who are you?"

"You don't want to know."

"Yes I do."

Nervously she twisted a lock of her long blond hair. Finally she whispered, "I am Garbage."

BRIGGS slept badly, in a sleeping bag under the left wing of the *Manta*. Pain kept him awake. His battered body, particularly his throbbing head, could find no comfortable position on the dune though he tossed and turned for hours. He finally dozed off, only to be brought back to consciousness by the first light of dawn. He watched the sky grow brighter and thought about things.

He had been dreaming about the attack on the *Corregidor,* about the explosion that had been almost the first warning of the Lorns' attack. There had been a violent shock and then a rush of air as the cabin atmosphere was sucked out through the punctured canopy. Briggs had held his breath and dived into a closet, a little compartment where tools were kept, then slammed the door behind him. The compartment had not been air tight, but it had retained enough air—and retained it long enough—so Briggs was still alive when his rescuers cut through the back of the closet.

In his dream, as in the actual event, everyone else in the control room had done nothing to save themselves. Briggs remembered their expressions. Some were surprised, some barely beginning to be afraid, but the overall impression was one of an unearthly peace: a detachment, a passivity. There were other closets opening onto the bridge, other near-air-tight chests and compartments available, but only Briggs had made a move to get into one. Everyone else had been . . . philosophical.

To Briggs this brief incident, when he had lived and everyone else on the bridge died, summed up his whole experience. The other officers had died with dignity. Briggs had scrambled for safety like a panicked chimpanzee and had survived.

Briggs had cared.

The others, deep down, had not.

When he'd gone to the meeting of the surviving officers he'd found them seriously planning to blow up the ship.

Once men had been different: when the domain of humanity was expanding; when each day brought news of some new planet colonized, some new alien race defeated. Now men asked whether humanity had any right to those hard-won colonies, whether it was worthwhile to go out among the stars and struggle for mastery of the galaxy. Perhaps, it was said, men should stay home, find inner peace through meditation (or at least pleasure through drugs, sex and luxury); perhaps it was even immoral to struggle.

Perhaps it was immoral to care what happened to the human race.

But Briggs cared.

At that moment, as he looked up at the stars that now grew faint with the approach of dawn, Briggs felt a terrible aloneness. Was he the only one who cared? If that was so, maybe it was no use going on. Briggs could give up. Without him, his crew would certainly give up. If other crews also gave up, humanity, without the protection of the starfleet, would have little choice but to give up. But what did it matter?

After Man was gone, the Lorns would mind the store.

Briggs buried his face in his hands, fighting an enemy he'd fought so many times before, an enemy more deadly than any Lorn . . . himself.

Once again he won.

He crept out of his sleeping bag and shuffled across the sand toward where the girl who called herself "Garbage" was sitting up and rubbing her eyes, childlike, with the backs of her fists. A few paces from her a guard stood at ease, watching her without interest.

Briggs crouched on his haunches beside her.

"Good morning, young lady."

"When will we eat?"

"Soon, my dear, soon. But while we're waiting I thought you and I might have a little chat."

"Eat first, then talk." She was pouting.

"We'll have breakfast soon enough." Briggs could hear sounds of movement inside the *Manta*. "Tell me, do you have any family?"

She shook her head, her long blond hair swishing. "No. No family."

"Any friends?"

"No."

"Is there anyone else living in that city?" He gestured toward the silent walls that now seemed almost to glow in the early morning light.

"No. I was alone."

"But how did you survive all alone like that?"

She shrugged. "I killed small animals. Sometimes I found things in cans. There is water in the wells."

"Amazing! And that was enough for you?"

Again she shrugged. "I am Garbage."

"Who gave you that name?"

"I gave it to myself. I have no other. When there is something that nobody wants, that's garbage, isn't it?"

"Are you something nobody wants?"

"Once I lived with the rulers. They tried to kill me. They did not want me." She glanced at the *Manta* with a worried frown. "They hunted me with flying machines."

"We won't hunt you," he reassured her.

"I believe you . . . since you have not killed me when you could. If you had come from them and had found my hiding place here, I would be dead by now."

Briggs paused, uncertain how to proceed. At last he said, "Do you know where these rulers live?"

"Of course. Once it was my home, but I will never again——"

"Will you lead me to it?"

Her eyes widened. "Don't ask me that!"

"Why not?"

"The Ecolog! She is so powerful! She is 300 years old, yet still young. She will never die. And she has absolute control!"

"Nevertheless," Briggs said grimly, "we must go to her."

BRIGGS ordered the crew of the *Manta* to open up all the parachutes on board and make clothing and tents suitable for a long desert trek. Mike Phillips began by carefully cutting out a dress for the girl called Garbage. It was light and white and loose-fitting, little more than a long rectangle of cloth with a hole cut in it for the head and a sash of the same nylon material to hold it in at the waist; plain and styleless, yet perfect for the environment.

He went on to make similar garments for himself. Garbage, wearing her new clothes, stood over him and watched as he worked in the shadow of the ship's wing. Finally she said, "I wish I could do that."

Mike glanced up at her with surprise. "Didn't you ever learn things like this?"

She shook her head. "Oh no. At court all our clothes were made by machines."

Mike ruefully examined his handiwork. "I'm sure they did a better job than I can. We don't have any needles or thread, let alone sewing machines or fabric melders. Even if we had them they wouldn't work without power."

She sighed. "Making clothing looks so difficult. I suppose only men can do it, not women."

"Why, that's not so. Anyone can do it. There was a time when it was considered exclusively women's work. Can you cook?"

"Cook?" She looked puzzled.

She didn't know the meaning of the word.

He said, "You know, can you prepare food for eating?"

"I can kill small animals," she answered brightly. "I kill them, tear them apart, then eat them. Is that what you mean?"

"Aren't they too tough to eat?"

"I got used to it. The food at court was better. Machines made the food at court, and men controlled the machines. Men are clever with their hands; they are good at keeping machines running."

Mike's square-cut features darkened into a frown. "Wait a minute. I don't understand. If women don't sew or cook, do they take care of children?"

"Oh no. Men and machines do that too."

"Then what do women do?"

"Why, they give commands, of course!" She began to giggle.

Mike bent to his work, now cutting out hoods and capes for himself and the girl. After a few minutes' silence, he said, "If women were the rulers at court, as you say, why did you leave?"

She sat down on the sand, not looking at him. "I had to leave. They were going to kill me."

"Kill you? Why?"

"I was not good enough."

"How were you different from the others?"

"I don't know. It seems to me I was exactly the same." She laid a particular stress on the word "exactly." Then she raised her head and regarded him seriously as she went on, "Others like me had been killed. The Ecolog does the killing herself, with a jewel-hilted sword. I was next. I slipped out of the court city, down the mountains. The Ecolog's men followed me in flying machines. They shot at me, but missed. I kept on, hiding in the daytime, traveling at night, until I came to the town where you found me. No people lived in the town. It had been abandoned, but there was canned food left behind and some gardens."

"Why did all the people leave?"

"The Ecolog commanded them to leave, of course. The city was becoming, I suppose, ecologically untenable. So many cities do that. One after another the cities are being abandoned." Her voice had become dreamy, faraway, but now her tone hardened abruptly. "One day I was treated like a princess, the next hunted like an animal. The Ecolog has no right to treat me like that." She laid her hand on his arm. "Your leader, Briggs, is a most powerful person, is he not?"

"In his way. . . ."

"Even though he is a man, he commands like an Ecolog."

Mike gave an ironic chuckle. "He commands, all right."

"Do you suppose he might be powerful enough to . . . to defeat the Ecolog, to kill her?"

"It's possible, but I don't think that's what he has in mind."

"Still, it might be arranged." She withdrew her hand from his arm, but her voice was gentle as she continued, "Do you know? I feel somehow I was born to rule, to command, just like your leader and the Ecolog."

Mike looked at her small sun-browned body and could not repress a smile.

She said scornfully. "You think I'm crazy, don't you? This man Briggs has asked me to lead him to the Ecolog. Up to this very minute I had been planning to pretend to lead him there, then, the moment he was off guard, I was going to slip away and leave him without a guide in the desert." Mike found her laugh somewhat disturbing. "But now I've changed my mind. I will lead him where he wants to go. Yes, and then see what happens."

She laughed again and Mike, in spite of the steadily rising temperature of the desert, felt for an instant a cold chill.

BRIGGS and the crew had been sleeping in shifts through the day. Now, as the sun lay low near the horizon and their shadows stretched long across the red dunes, he checked to see that all was ready. Having scuffed out a message in the sand for the *Corregidor*, he ordered his little caravan to move.

Briggs, Phillips and the girl walked side by side in the lead; the others fell into rough formation behind, two abreast.

"Shouldn't we leave someone to guard the *Manta*?" Mike asked, with a worried glance over his shoulder.

Briggs snorted. "Without power, the *Manta*'s no more

than a pile of useless scrap. Do you want me to weaken this already pitiful exploratory force just to guard a scrapheap?"

"I suppose not, sir," Phillips replied glumly.

In the gathering darkness they trudged through the abandoned city. By the time they reached the gate at the opposite end of the main street, the last trace of sunlight had vanished. They paused to check their gear. (Each man carried an improvised backpack containing food, equipment and—most important—water.)

When they were under way again, marching out across the open sand, Mike said to Garbage, "I don't see any road from here on."

She answered lightly, "There isn't any. Once there was a road, but now the sand has covered it."

Mike felt vaguely uneasy. "With no road, how will you find your way?"

She gestured heavenward. "I can never get lost while I can see the Great Whirlpool."

Above, the sky was filled with the spiral nebula.

HOURS later Briggs broke the long silence. "She's right, you know, Mister Phillips."

Slightly startled, Phillips said, "About what, sir?"

The commodore nodded toward the nebula. "About the so-called Great Whirlpool up there. As long as we can see that, we're not completely lost."

The girl had been walking slightly faster than the rest of the caravan and now was some distance ahead. Briggs said, "She was speaking of directions down here on the ground. I'm talking about something more. That's the good old Milky Way Galaxy up there, isn't it?"

"I suppose so," Phillips answered without conviction.

"Of course it is. We didn't fly long enough to reach any other galaxy. So we can be pretty damn sure we're still in the Milky Way system, but it's also obvious we're far out of the galactic plane. Now are we above or below the plane, eh?"

Mike felt annoyed. "How should I know? I'm not an astrogator." It seemed to him the galaxy would look exactly the same from the top and bottom.

"I'm not an astrogator either," said Briggs. "But I know the answer anyway. Think, man."

"I'm sorry. I don't know."

"We're below the plane, of course. If we were above the plane the spiral would turn counterclockwise, but it's turning clockwise, you see?"

Grudgingly Mike agreed.

"And you be damn glad we live in a spiral galaxy, not a ring-shaped or ball-shaped one. That kind really would look the same from the top and bottom. But now we can't be altogether outside the system, can we, since the spiral fills the sky? We're narrowing things down."

"To a few billion light-years," said Mike glumly.

"Don't be defeatist. Look here, if we were to view the galaxy from directly below, it would look pretty much as if it was a regular golden section spiral inscribed on a circle. Now look up there. Is that a circle?"

"No, more of an oval."

"An oval you say? Right! So that means we're not beneath the center of the spiral. We're some distance toward the edge. I'd say we're viewing the spiral hub from about a ten-degree angle to the galactic plane. Right?"

"If you say so."

"I do say so." Briggs sounded disgustingly smug. "That would put us, all things considered, more than halfway out from the hub of the galaxy, but less than a quarter of the way to the rim."

Mike realized that with each observation Briggs was eliminating a vast number of possibilities, but here it seemed Briggs must stop. "That's pretty good, as far as it goes," said Mike.

"Ah, but I'm not finished yet. Did we fly at near light speed long enough to cross the galaxy? We did not. Therefore we can be sure we're not on the other side of the hub. I think we've narrowed our position down to an arc of about 20 degrees horizontally and ten degrees vertically. Not a bad neighborhood." The commodore was searching the sky eagerly.

"Now what are you looking for?" Mike demanded.

"The White Giants! You've got younger eyes than mine. Help me look. Right around there somewhere." He pointed.

Mike looked, but it was Briggs who found them. He spoke with a kind of awe. "There they are, Altair and Sirius. They don't look like much from here, but they're the brightest things within 20 light-years of Earth." He was pointing at two gleaming points of light near the end of one of the arms of the spiral nebula. "You can't see our own sun—good old Sol—from here of course, but it's there! It's about two-thirds of the way along a line drawn from Altair to Sirius, as seen from this angle. Altair is 16 light-years from Earth; Sirius is only eight point seven." Mike noticed the commodore's voice was shaking.

Mike looked away, embarrassed.

He was, nevertheless, impressed. The commodore, without instruments, without even a telescope, had found the way home.

The sky began to brighten.

The Great Whirlpool faded. A large portion of it had already passed below the horizon.

With surprising speed the desert became visible around them, taking on muted color. No sign of the city lay behind them, no sign of anything else ahead. There was nothing but sand in all directions.

Briggs raised his hand. The caravan halted. "Did you hear something?" the commodore whispered.

Everyone listened intently.

The silence was broken by Garbage, up ahead of the rest of them. "I hear it! I hear it!" Undisguised fear was in her voice. She turned and ran toward Briggs and Phillips, white garments swirling behind her, bare feet kicking up little clouds of dust.

Phillips could hear it now, the faint distant drone and flutter of some sort of motor.

Garbage clutched Mike's arm with fingers that dug into the flesh and screamed, "The Ecolog! The Ecolog!"

During the moments before the sun broke the horizon, the huge, silver dirigible, like a mirage, passed slowly in the distance.

CHAPTER 5

Sunrise; an early morning of majestic splendor began in a hush.

Under a sky of muted blue, the horizon filled to a great height with a greenish golden haze that hinted of distant mountains whose shapes could not be seen clearly enough to be certain of their reality. The dunes, however, remained gray and somehow ghostly, a sandy garment carelessly dropped by a giant, a garment that draped its folds from horizon to horizon.

Out of the haze, quite suddenly, came a stabbing ray of unbearable light. The sun had made its entrance, and having entered, grew. It was at first an inverted dish, viewed edge-on, then, climbing higher, it became a bowl, till, clearing the skyline, a bloated reddish-white egg formed. The men could still see their breath—brief white clouds in the cold air—but the sun's heat already made itself unmistakably felt on their sunward side.

Frowning, Briggs surveyed the far haze. Was that a harmless cloud, or a sandstorm? He could not say. He turned to his little caravan. "We'll pitch camp here. Dig in as well as you can." He spoke softly, as though in a cathedral.

The tents went up, white against the shadowed tan of the dunes. Would these makeshift shelters last more than a few seconds in a real wind? The commodore shaded his eyes and looked up.

Perhaps at this instant the *Corregidor* was passing overhead. The techmen might be watching him on a video-telescope. Yes, they could see him even if he could not see them. He wondered if he should try to communicate with them, but decided his presence here was self-explanatory.

Once, long ago, men had feared the void of outer space.

Now, he thought, we know the real dangers are down here.

THE sandstorm did not materialize, but as the sun neared the zenith the temperature rose to a point that rendered sleep impossible. To lie still was an agony; yet movement also was slow and painful. Commodore Briggs made a decision. They would push on now and rest later, after sundown.

They folded their tents and straggled onward, Garbage leading the way, navigating by the sun.

The desert had become unreal, shimmering, too bright to look at. Part of the time Briggs marched with eyes closed. It was not necessary to make much use of the sense of sight. There were no obstacles to avoid, no path to follow, no hiding places where enemies might lie in wait.

It seemed to him he could have found his way by the sense of hearing, which told him where the rest of his squad was, and his sense of heat, which told him where the sun was.

He slogged forward through a red universe as the sunlight through his closed eyelids created shining geometrical patterns, and sometimes grotesque leering faces, on his retinas.

When he opened his eyes momentarily, Briggs noticed that Garbage was wearing an odd pair of glasses she'd apparently fashioned from bits of material cannibalized from the Manta. They were nothing more than a bit of cardboard that fitted over the bridge of the nose with a narrow slit in front of the eyes. He vaguely remembered that skiers wore some such things to prevent snow blindness.

So, the girl was the only person in this caravan who could really see. Briggs did not like that. Yet the terrible heat seemed to paralyze his mind. He could not think of anything to do about it or summon the will to take any action. He was totally absorbed in placing one foot in front of the other.

He opened his eyes again for an instant. There was the girl, leading the procession. Her steps were not sluggish, but quick and lively. The dunes were not her enemy, but her home. And it was she, Briggs realized, who now commanded. Naturally, without effort, she had taken over.

He felt for the handle of his sword, as if afraid he might have lost it, and with it his position of authority. It was still there, thank God! It hung in its scabbard the same as always; yet, in this situation, what meaning did it have? Damn little!

It was late afternoon when one of the men fainted.

The caravan stopped for a while, and attempts were made to revive him, but he did not regain consciousness.

Briggs turned to the girl and asked, "You know the desert. What can we do for him?"

"Cut his throat," she answered lightly.

"Be serious."

"I am being serious. If you leave him behind he will die. If you try to carry him along, those who have to carry him will soon also faint. If you cannot bring yourself to kill him, if he is your close friend or something, I will do the job for you."

There was a long silence. Then Briggs said, "We'll make camp here."

Garbage said, "I think I should tell you we are being followed."

Briggs looked up, startled. "Followed?"

"By animals. They have been trailing us for hours. They think some of us may die. If you leave them a man they will gorge themselves and let the rest of us alone."

"And if we don't?"

She shrugged. "Perhaps they will attack, perhaps not. It depends how hungry they are. Leave them a man. Better they should have one of us than all of us."

"We're armed," said Briggs.

"Can you see in the dark?" asked the girl softly. "The animals can. They can see heat as clearly as you see light. And soon it will be night."

Briggs looked back the way they had come. He could see nothing, only shimmering brightness and endless sand. Was she lying? He had no way of knowing.

He turned toward Phillips and growled, "Can't you get that man on his feet?"

Mike shook his head.

"Rig a stretcher," the commodore commanded.

"Out of what?" asked the girl in a mocking tone.

They had no poles, no rifles, nothing that would serve the purpose. Briggs felt dizzy. His mind refused to function. "All right, dammit. We'll take turns carrying him. Nobody take him more than a little way."

The girl said with contempt, "You fool."

Briggs took the first turn carrying the unconscious soldier over his shoulders. He had to set an example for the men, didn't he? The soldier was heavy, impossibly heavy. Briggs lurched from side to side like a drunk. Ahead he heard the girl's light, quick footsteps; behind, the panting and sighs of his men. He did not open his eyes until he heard her shout, "Look there!"

He blinked, followed the line of her gaze to his left. In the whiteness something moved, then was still.

"It's one of the animals," said the girl soberly. "They're coming closer, trying to encircle us."

Briggs squinted for a long time, but whatever that had been moving out there was now invisible.

It was Mike's turn to carry the soldier.

The sun had gone; the nebula returned, and its blue light turned the desert into a vague pattern of soft-edged shadows. The temperature was falling fast. Briggs could think again, but his body was dead tired.

And now that he could see, he had spotted the creatures several times. They seemed about the size and shape of

wolves, but appeared to have little or no fur and an extra
pair of legs. They moved fast, darting from shadow to
shadow. He fired at one with his stinger pistol, but it did
not fall.

"They have armor on their bodies," explained the girl.
"We call them ngaas." (The "ng" sound was pronounced
as in "wing" and "sing.") Briggs thought, *What kind of
armor can stop a rocket dart?*

The ngaa scuttled again from one dune to another, now
looking more like some immense spider than any sort of
canine. Another ngaa appeared, then disappeared. Then
yet another.

"How intelligent are they?" Briggs asked her.

"Not as intelligent as men, but they have a language.
Before humans came to this planet, they were the highest
form of life here. We thought they'd become extinct when
the Ecolog changed the ecology, but it seems some have
survived and adapted to the new environment. Every
year they become more of a problem." She raised her finger
to her lips. "Hush! You can hear them."

Briggs strained his ears.

At first there was nothing; but soon he could make out
a faint hissing, whistling and clicking.

"You see?" she said. "They're talking . . . about us."

Briggs said, "Can you understand what they're saying?"

She shook her head and laughed contemptuously. "Of
course not!"

The rustle of the ngaas grew louder; they began to
sound like a vast, whispering crowd.

Garbage said uneasily, "There are so many of them. I
don't know if one man will satisfy them."

Briggs said, "They won't get even one, if I have anything to say about it."

The ngaas were getting so close now that Briggs could
hear their scampering feet. He could even smell them.
They had a sharp, pungent odor, not altogether unpleas-

ant. In fact at first it seemed rather sweet when it was faint and far-off and he caught it in scattered whiffs. But when the sluggish breeze shifted slightly the odor became abruptly much stronger, so Briggs could literally taste it as well as smell it. Then the sweetness became sickening: raw, rancid, sensual, crude, intoxicating. It made him dizzy, nauseous.

He thought of roses rotting in the rain, of roses piled in an open grave: billions and billions of decaying roses. Sweet, sweet, poisonously sweet. He was suffocating, choking on that malodorous, fetid, foul, putrid, pink sweetness.

Without warning the ngaas fell silent.

Their reek remained, but the creatures could no longer be seen or heard.

"They hear something," whispered the girl.

Briggs heard it too. It was the unmistakable fluttering roar of the dirigible. He looked in the direction of the sound and saw, against the starry background, a tiny moving point of light. How slowly it moved!

"Flashlights!" commanded Briggs. "Turn on every flashlight we have. Wave them around! Shout! Jump up and down! We must attract those people's attention."

"No!" protested the girl. "No! You fools!"

They did not listen to her. Even though weary and half-dead, the little party somehow found the energy to break into a wild, shouting, light-waving dance.

"They're coming this way!" exclaimed one of the soldiers.

He was right. The moving point of light grew brighter; the motor sounded louder. The dirigible was definitely coming closer.

"Help!" bellowed Briggs. "We're right down here! Help! Help!"

Mike Phillips, behind him, held the unconscious soldier, but managed a healthy shout.

The dirigible became clearer every minute.

The one light had become many, and the gasbag blocked out the stars in a dark oval. Briggs realized that this time the airship would pass directly overhead.

"Help!" he screamed hoarsely. "Help!"

The roar of the motors had become deafening. Could his cries for help be heard over that roar? Probably not, but Briggs shouted all the louder!

Suddenly the ship turned slightly and Briggs could see banks of floor-to-ceiling windows in the gondola of the vessel. There were people inside, men and women dressed in bright flowing robes and jewels. They were chatting, smoking, drinking cocktails. None of them were looking out the windows.

"Help!" screamed Briggs.

The ship passed directly above his head, drifting slightly sideways.

It passed and continued on its way.

Briggs was the last to stop yelling, the last to lower his flashlight and snap it off.

Garbage said bitterly, "If they'd stopped, it would only have been to watch the ngaas eat us."

With the fading of the motor drone, the rustle of the scampering ngaas recommenced. One of the soldiers beamed his flashlight into the gloom and picked out a pair of glittering eyes.

"Commodore Briggs," said Mike uncomfortably.

"What is it, Lieutenant?" snapped Briggs.

Mike nodded at the man draped over his shoulders. "This soldier has stopped breathing, sir. I think he's dead."

Briggs stepped quickly over and took the man's pulse. There was no pulse. The wrist was cold to the touch. Briggs said, "He's been dead for some time."

"We'd better bury him, sir," said Phillips. "Don't want the ngaas to get him."

Garbage let out a wordless howl of protest and dashed forward to throw herself against Phillips, knocking the corpse to the ground.

"Leave him!" she shrieked. "Where do you think you are? Leave him! It's our only chance!"

Ignoring her, Mike stooped to pick up the body.

Briggs raised his hand. "Wait. She's right." His voice was almost a whisper. "Leave him."

The soldiers stared at him, but obeyed.

The procession trudged onward, leaving the dead man spread-eagled on the sand. Briggs tried not to listen to the awful crunching and munching in the darkness behind him.

HOURS passed.

Shortly before dawn Briggs called a halt.

He turned to the girl. "Have you seen anything of the ngaas?"

She shook her head. "I think one man was enough for them. They probably won't bother us again."

"Probably?"

"You can never be sure."

He nodded. "I see. Then we'd better bed down here and try to grab some sleep while we can."

Phillips said, "We have only three more days before the energy on the *Corregidor* is used up."

Briggs sighed. "I know, I know. But we have to rest sometime."

The commodore assigned two men to sentry duty and, totally exhausted, fell into a deep sleep. When the sentries were sure everyone was asleep, they stopped pacing and sat down.

Said one, "I can watch just as easily sitting down as standing up."

"Me too," said the other.

Ten minutes later, both were asleep.

Thus no one was awake to hear the stealthy rustle of something moving toward them, slowly and carefully, through the darkness.

CHAPTER 6

At first Briggs was aware only of a sensation of heat. It was a sensation he now knew well. Even with eyes closed he could feel the position of the sun not far above the horizon. The warmth was welcome after the cold of the night; his body was stiff, partly from the night chill and partly from the hardness of his sand-dune bed. *It's morning*, he thought, and rolled over, reluctant to begin the day, reluctant to open his eyes. Around him he could hear the other men beginning to stir. Then he frowned. *Why isn't anyone shaking us awake? The sentries....* Cautiously he opened his eyes a crack.

Standing over him, sword in hand, was a short, dark-skinned man in loose-fitting burnoose, tunic and ballooning white trousers. The man was smiling, but not in a friendly manner.

"Ah, I see you are awake," said the man softly.

He nudged Briggs in the ribs with a sandaled foot, lifting the sword ever-so-slightly as if to say, "Don't try anything." Briggs sat up, careful not to make any sudden moves.

The man went on in a mocking tone, "I have your sword, and your other weapons too, so it would be foolish of you to give us any trouble."

Briggs glanced around. Other burnoose-clad, desert-bronzed little men were standing over the members of his party, including the two sentries. The sentries turned away, ashamed to look Briggs in the eye. "Your guards were asleep," the stranger explained. "Bad discipline." The mocking smile broadened.

How true, thought Briggs. There was a time when men were shot by a firing squad for less. Things had changed.

One of the sentries whispered, "Sorry, sir."

"Who are you?" Briggs asked, turning his attention to his captor.

"I am called Sewall," the muscular little man answered. "I'm a scout for the city of Arbre."

"The city of Arbre?"

"Over there." Sewall pointed toward the horizon.

Briggs stared in the direction indicated and saw a range of mountains not far away. Perhaps this was what he'd dimly seen the day before, but had mistaken for a sandstorm.

"You live in the mountains?" Briggs asked.

"No. The Ecolog lives in the mountains. We live in the jungle at the foot of the mountains."

Briggs squinted. Yes, indeed, a city was there, half-hidden in distant greenery. It was, like the abandoned city in the desert, surrounded by a high white wall. Briggs asked, "Are you taking us there?"

"That's right. Now, on your feet!"

Briggs obeyed, and the rest of his party followed his example. The last to stand was Garbage. Sewall scowled at her and grunted, "What are you doing still alive?"

She replied bitterly. "Would it make you feel better if I killed myself here and now?"

Sewall raised his sword. "That's an excellent idea; but unfortunately I'm under orders to bring you all to Arbre alive, so march!"

They marched.

Waiting for them beyond the next dune was a small herd of horselike animals, apparently native to the planet. The animals were six-legged and three-eyed and scaled like reptiles. Sewall spoke to the creatures in a whistling, twittering language, to which they replied sullenly. Sewall translated, chuckling, "They don't like your smell." He grinned at Briggs.

The feeling was mutual. The creatures had a cheap rose perfume smell not unlike that of the ngaas.

"Mount up," Sewall commanded, indicating the saddle and stirrups each animal wore. Briggs stepped into a stirrup and swung into the saddle. The creature craned its skinny neck around and regarded him with three red eyes full of undisguised hostility. "Easy, boy," Briggs murmured soothingly. The creature answered with a few contemptuous monosyllables.

When everyone was mounted, Sewall gave an order in creature-language, and the procession set off in the direction of Arbre.

In spite of a rather ungainly appearance, the creatures were remarkably fast. They had no reins—none were needed since they responded perfectly to verbal commands in their own language—and Briggs found himself clinging for dear life to a kind of handlebar on the front of his saddle. The wind whipped through his desert garb, causing his cloak to stream out behind him as he lurched forward and back, forward and back. Briggs began to feel somewhat ill and Sewall, noticing his discomfort, only laughed.

"If you join us, we'll teach you to ride," called the little brown man, and for the first time his voice held a hint of warmth.

Less than an hour had passed, according to Briggs's guess, when the dead sands of the desert were quite abruptly behind them. They found themselves galloping along a wide, two-lane dirt road between broad expanses of green, irrigated fields. Men in dirty-white burnooses worked rhythmically and sang. The agriculture was primitive, Briggs realized. On an advanced planet all the crops would have been in kilometer after kilometer of plastic-covered terrariums. With terrarium agriculture, food could be grown almost anywhere, even in the desert, on a fraction of the water needed for open-air agriculture, and with no danger from pests.

Briggs nodded with satisfaction. Everything fitted the pattern he had suspected almost from the first. The Ecolog might have a technology in some ways more advanced than his own, but she was keeping it to herself.

Ahead loomed the vast city gates. At a shouted password from Sewall, the massive wood doors swung open to allow them to pass. A moment later Briggs was thundering along a wide, paved street where vendors and townspeople scrambled to get out of his way. *How to stay in power?* Briggs was thinking. *Just make sure you're the only one who knows how things work.* In the nineteenth and twentieth centuries the great powers of the northern hemisphere had used a similar strategy to keep what was called "The Third World" in its place.

In fact, with no great effort of the imagination, Briggs could visualize himself back on Earth, before the space age, somewhere below the Tropic of Cancer—in Africa, South America, or Vietnam—perhaps in Southern India with a head full of spiritual values and a belly full of nothing. The city of Arbre could have come from the past in some immense time machine.

The only thing that didn't fit was the animals.

On Earth the beasts of burden and the house pets did not have six or eight legs. On Earth, animals did not, as they obviously did here, converse with each other and with their masters in a highly developed if nonhuman language. But even back on Earth the animals had been citizens of human civilization, though they occupied the lowest rung of the social ladder.

The sickly sweet rose smell of the alien animals was everywhere, dominating even the smell of dung and rancid vegetable oil; their twittering and squeaking could be heard mingling with the vendors' cries and children's screams and workers' curses. It was impossible to tell which group was more numerous; the humans or the aliens. *And,* thought Briggs uncomfortably, *who am I to call those beings aliens? After all, they were here first.*

Briggs's steed halted so suddenly that Briggs was almost thrown from the saddle. The other steeds gathered in a

milling crowd in what appeared to be the city's central
square. One of the creatures spoke to another with what
sounded like sarcasm. Briggs asked Garbage, "What are
they saying?"

With a toss of the head she replied, "How should I
know? Am I a townie?"

Sewall moved alongside, saying angrily, "Who are you
calling a townie?"

With false sweetness she replied, "Everyone else but
you."

He growled, "A remark like that could cost you your
life."

"If you were going to kill me, you'd have done it
already," she pointed out with the same false sweetness.

He glared at her a moment before shouting, "Dismount!"

THEY had ascended a broad marble staircase and now
were entering the echoing vastness of a dim, high-vaulted
hallway. Sewall led the way, with Commodore Briggs,
Lieutenant Phillips and Garbage right behind. The rest
followed.

Briggs noted that, in spite of his muscular body and
commanding manner, there was something feminine about
Sewall, something delicate and fastidious. With a con-
noisseur's smile, Sewall was studying the ornate floral
patterns carved into the walls they were passing. Was this
man an architect, or an artist, or both?

Briggs remarked, "Beautiful workmanship."

Sewall nodded, pleased. "It's 100 years old," he said,
as proudly as if he'd made the designs himself.

They ascended another flight of marble stairs.

Briggs noted that the wall decorations had become
cruder, uglier, more amateurish. He asked Sewall, "Are
these designs earlier?"

Sewall turned and stopped walking. In the dim light,
his face was clouded and defensive. "No, later." He

gestured toward the walls. "This is all modern work here . . . contemporary."

In Briggs's mind another piece of the puzzle fell into place. He smiled faintly. Yes, in more ways than one Arbre could have been transported here by some time machine from twentieth-century Earth.

Presently, they halted before a heavy, dark-stained wood door. Two white-burnoosed guards stood at attention, one on each side of the doorway. They were armed with steel-tipped spears.

Sewall's voice fell to a whisper. "This is the office of our Lord Mayor, the Right Honorable Broog Mano." He addressed one of the guards. "I am Scout Sewall. I have prisoners for the Lord Mayor's questioning."

The guard replied in a bored tone, "The outlanders?"

"Yes."

"They are expected. Bring them in."

The second guard opened the door and stood aside for Sewall, Briggs, Phillips and Garbage. "The rest of you wait outside," said the first guard. The way was suddenly blocked by their spears.

When the door had shut behind him, Sewall said respectfully, "Lord Mayor?"

A curtain parted at the back of the shadowed room and a tall, black-robed man appeared. Briggs had a glimpse of something behind the curtain, something that strongly resembled a large shortwave radio set; then the heavy drape fell back in place, concealing this apparently secret piece of anachronistic equipment.

"Ah, Scout Sewall," said the Lord Mayor, walking slowly forward. The Lord Mayor was a dignified man in his seventies, almost bald but for a fringe of gray hair. "You have done well."

Sewall grinned, "Thank you, sir." For a moment the little man looked very much like a pleased teenager.

Lord Mayor Mano extended his hand to Briggs, saying,

"Welcome to Arbre. Is there anything I can get for you?"

They shook hands. Briggs was surprised by the sudden hospitality, but he answered without thinking, "You can give me back my claymore."

Mano frowned, puzzled. "Claymore?"

"My sword."

Mano turned toward Sewall and said, "Give the man his sword, please."

Sewall was flustered. "But your honor—"

"Give it to him."

Sewall opened his cloak to produce the weapon and reluctantly handed it over.

"Thank you," said Briggs, slipping the blade into its scabbard.

Mano explained, "Scout Sewall disarmed you for your own good. You might have done yourself injury in trying to escape, might even have died in the desert. Actually we have only the most friendly of intentions toward you."

"Indeed?"

"Of course!"

"Then can we trouble you for a little time on your master computer?"

Mano looked blank. "Computer? What's a computer?"

"It's a machine that computes . . . does arithmetic."

Mano brightened. "Oh, I know what you mean. Wait a moment." The Lord Mayor disappeared behind his drapes. Briggs breathed a sigh of infinite relief and said to Mike, "It looks like things are going to be easy for once."

Mike grinned. "That'll be a change."

Lord Mayor Mano was also grinning as he reappeared from behind the curtain. "Here you are. My computer." With eager generosity, he offered Briggs a well-worn Chinese bead abacus.

MANO had led them out onto a broad balcony. The morning sun was blindingly bright after the dimness of the office. The Lord Mayor, with a note of awe in his voice, pointed a long finger toward the mountains. "That is the fortress of the Ecolog. If anyone knows about such things as computers, she does."

Shading his eyes with his hand, Briggs gazed upward. There, beyond the first range, well above the tree line—in fact on the peak of the highest mountain in sight—was a silver tower, a squat, domed building and an irregularly shaped wall. These structures were too far away for him to make out any details, but Briggs received an impression of advanced scientific building techniques. And that dome . . . was it made from solid gold?

At his elbow, Garbage muttered, "It wasn't easy to get down from there. I don't know if it's possible to get up."

"We'll find a way," said Briggs firmly. He turned to Mano and added, "Lord Mayor, can you send the Ecolog a radio message for us?"

The man turned pale. "I cannot call her. It is she who calls me."

"This is an exception."

"There are no exceptions." With effort, Mano got a grip on himself. "She will call soon I'm sure, and then we can bring up any questions you might have—tactfully of course."

Briggs cocked his head to one side. "Tell me, sir. If something goes wrong with your radio, how do you repair it?"

The old man seemed surprised by the question. "I don't repair it. Nobody in the city of Arbre can repair a radio. The Ecolog sends someone."

Briggs nodded thoughtfully. "I see. Be frank now. Don't you sometimes resent being so totally dependent?"

"Not at all. The secrets of electric things are known only to the Ecolog and to her court, and that is the way it should be. If everyone had such knowledge, there would be competition, perhaps war. This way we always have peace. And we are protected from each other, from the outsiders."

"Like us?" Briggs demanded.

"No offense intended. We mean you no harm."

Garbage added derisively, "The Ecolog tells you what to plant and when, what to make and how much, even who to marry and how many children to have. What a relief it must be never to have to decide about anything!"

The Lord Mayor snapped, "I won't take that from your kind!"

The girl answered sharply, "What kind is that? Don't you know I used to live in that castle up there on the mountain?"

"Yes, of course. But you were cast out, rejected."

"But why? Why was I cast out?"

Mano seemed confused. "I don't know. You must have been imperfect in some way."

"Imperfect?" The girl was frowning. "But I was exactly like all the others."

Mano became self-assured, even pompous. "I'm sure there was something. The Ecolog has reasons for everything she does. She's not like you and me. She's 300 years old, yet still young and beautiful. She'll never grow any older. She has the wisdom of the old and the brightness of the young, both at the same time. And since she will never die, her mind is not clouded by the fears that plague mortals. She is beautiful, too. She's the most beautiful woman who ever—"

Garbage broke in. "If she's so beautiful why does she wear a mask? She could be a monster and nobody would know."

Mano was aghast at this suggestion. "Blasphemy! Blasphemy!"

Sewall joined in the conversation, his voice teasing, ironic. "The girl may be right. The mask is beautiful, with all the platinum and jewels and everything, but who can say what's behind the mask? There are times when she certainly acts like a monster."

"I'm warning you, Sewall." said Mano.

"Warning me? You cannot frighten a man who has faced a pack of hungry ngaas in the dunes at night. We owe these strangers nothing; but we would be poor hosts if we did not at least give them the truth. We have nothing to lose." The little man turned to face Briggs. "Once a man built an outhouse where it might pollute a public well. She ran him through with that jeweled sword of hers. Once a woman gave birth to three children instead of the legal two. The Ecolog slit the throat of the extra child and the doctors sterilized the mother. And when a child is feeble-minded, deformed or sickly—"

Mano protested, "It is not for us to judge the Ecolog. She is all-wise, all-knowing!"

"Is she?" said Sewall. "Or is she merely all-powerful?"

Briggs said dryly, "No mere human is all-powerful."

"But," Sewall persisted, "a human can become so powerful nobody dares oppose her."

Mano said stiffly, "That's treasonous talk, Sewall."

"Treasonous?" The little scout's tone was unctuous. "Not at all! I am Her Majesty's most loyal servant." He bowed. "But, unlike most citizens of Arbre, I insist on serving with open eyes." He became more serious. "There may once have been a time when revolt against the Ecolog was possible, but that time is now long past. Only fools dream of the impossible! Isn't that right, my Lord Mayor Mano?"

The mayor had been glancing around uneasily as if searching for eavesdroppers. "Oh yes. That's right. Of course." With a pained expression, the old man turned to Briggs. "I hope this upstart's wild talk hasn't prejudiced you against us."

Briggs said curtly, "Would it matter if it had?"

"Well. . . ." Mano seemed to be having trouble getting to the point. "I want to extend to you an invitation—"

"Yes?" prompted Briggs.

"An invitation to become citizens of Arbre."

"All of us?" said Mike, surprised.

Mano pointed a shaking finger at Garbage. "All but her!"

Briggs answered grimly, "I'm sorry, but we cannot accept any invitations that do not include Miss Garbage. She has become a most valuable member of our crew."

The girl called Garbage stared at Briggs with astonished gratitude.

IN the temple Briggs received his first idea of the Ecolog's appearance. A statue of her stood behind an altar laden with offerings of food. As he approached the idol, Briggs walked slowly down the middle aisle of the huge, echoing, cathedrallike building, a puzzled scowl on his homely face, his bushy brows knitted together.

He stopped at the foot of the statue and peered up.

Lieutenant Phillips stood on his right, Garbage on his left, and Sewall the scout slightly ahead of him. The others followed, murmuring.

"Handsome woman, if this statue is a likeness," said the commodore softly. The image was sculpted from white marble, five times taller than a man. The Ecolog was portrayed in the posture of a loving mother, arms outspread to welcome in her children. The design and workmanship were of that masterly quality Briggs had learned to recognize as being at least 100 years old. Where arms, legs or neck emerged from her flowing classical robes, the painter had used great skill to imitate real flesh; it was easy to imagine that a genuine living giantess was standing here, waiting to embrace a multitude.

The only disturbing note was the mask.

The mask was made of polished metal, concealing the face from brows to chin except for the eyeslits. A pair of startlingly realistic blue eyes seemed to peer through, reflecting a beam of sunlight cleverly aimed to illuminate the head of the statue and nothing else. The cheeks of the mask were incised with an elaborate serpentine or perhaps floral pattern, and studded with many-colored, translucent jewels, which could have been intended to represent fruit or, equally well, the glittering eyes of snakes.

Briggs felt oddly ambivalent.

The Ecolog's slender girl-like form attracted him.

Her metal mask repelled him, inspired a trace of irrational, superstitious fear. Yet the mask, too, was beautiful in its way.

He asked Mike, "What's behind that mask, eh?"

Mike shrugged. "Beats me."

Briggs was depressed. The interview with the Lord Mayor had returned his claymore to him and, in a manner of speaking, he had been given the keys to the city, but he had not achieved the precious few minutes of computer time he needed. For that, it seemed, he would have to appeal to management.

Sewall said softly, mockingly, "Those who ask for nothing, get nothing."

Briggs spun around to face him, demanding, "Are you reading my mind?"

"Don't be absurd, Briggs."

"Then what did you mean by that?"

"Only that if you had persisted, our dear Lord Mayor would have allowed you to bring your garbage friend with you when you became a citizen of Arbre."

Briggs answered soberly, "None of us intend to become members of your community."

Sewall's eyebrows raised. "No?"

"No. We have to push on into the mountains as soon as possible."

"I understand," said Sewall. "You must go to the goddess. Only she can answer your prayers."

Briggs said sharply, "Your Ecolog is no goddess."

Sewall smiled like a leering leprechaun. "I know that. You know that. But the people who lay all these offerings before her statue . . . do they know that? But, very well.

I'll take you to the marketplace. You'll need steeds, mountain-climbing equipment. . . ." He had started for one of the side exits.

Following him, the commodore said, "And our stinger pistols."

Sewall answered with mock pity. "I'm so sorry, Mr. Briggs. Those weapons are too advanced to be allowed outside the court of the Ecolog. She will pick them up on her next visit."

"Now see here. . . ." Briggs had his hand on the pommel of his claymore.

"That's right," said the gleeful Sewall. "First kill me, then kill the temple guards, then the entire population of Arbre, if you think you can."

He led them through the exit, saying, with the air of a tourist guide, "We are now entering the famous Hall of Mummies."

Briggs glanced uneasily to his right, then to his left.

Along either side of the dim passageway stood, as if at attention, an honor guard of corpses. They were all, probably thanks to the dry desert air, remarkably well preserved. Only the hard grayness of the skin and the lack of movement betrayed the fact that they were not alive.

Sewall babbled on. "The mummies you see along the wall are of no importance. They're here for decoration, though if you don't find them decorative I'd have to agree with you. They're the unworthy ones, human garbage cast out by the Ecolog."

With a shudder, Briggs had already recognized the bodies when the girl named Garbage rushed to the wall and looked up at one of the silent figures. It was that of a young woman with long, blond hair dressed in a loose-fitting, white tunic.

Garbage said nothing for almost a full minute while Sewall watched her, a sly smirk on his face. At last, her skin pale, eyes wild, she turned and faced him. "It's me!" she screamed. "They're all me!"

It was true. Each and every one of the stiff, dry corpses was, at least at first glance, exactly alike, and all were the image of Garbage—two lines of her macabre duplicates stretching off into the dark distance.

THERE was a problem.

Commodore Briggs had no money to buy the equipment needed to climb the mountains. During lunch Sewall commiserated with him.

"It's all for the best," said the dark little man soothingly. "Life in Arbre may not be exciting, but it's better than no life at all. Those mountains are dangerous, you know. You could kill yourself trying to—"

Briggs grunted, "I can't stay here." He glanced around. They were sitting in a rather rough and decaying outdoor cafe, dirt-floored, with heavy, crude wooden tables and benches. Shade from the vicious sun was provided by a faded awning overhead. Also, somewhere overhead Briggs knew, was the *Corregidor* and the crew who depended on him.

Sewall, seated across the table, leaned forward and gestured toward Garbage. "Ah, but you can. Get rid of the girl."

"No."

Sewall shrugged. "All right. Keep her then, if you're willing to argue with the Ecolog about her. But you should realize that the Ecolog seldom loses an argument."

"Before I can argue with her, I have to speak to her."

"That can be arranged."

"When?"

"In a week or a month . . . she visits Arbre from time to time, but we never know in advance when she's coming."

"I need to speak to her now."

Sewall raised his hands in a gesture of resignation. "You must know that's impossible."

Mike Phillips, seated next to Briggs, put in, "We're not

familiar with your customs. We come from . . . quite a long way."

Sewall's interest perked up. "Oh? Do you come from the city of Droon?"

Mike shook his head. "No."

"Rahoor? Oowak? Wumdum? Wibblewak?"

Mike grinned. "No."

Briggs said, "We come from another planet."

Sewall burst out laughing. "Then you are outlanders indeed!"

Briggs was surprised. "Don't you believe me?"

"What do you take me for? If you come from some distant city that you'd rather not name, I won't press you, but don't tell me any tall tales about other planets. There are no other planets."

Briggs and Mike glanced at each other. Briggs said, "Your ancestors came here from another planet."

"That's a myth. The Ecolog tells us that to impress the superstitious masses, to make herself appear as the creator of our society. No intelligent man still believes those old stories. The human race evolved by a process of natural selection. That's what really happened."

Briggs said softly, "At night, when you look up into the sky, what do you see?"

"The Great Whirlpool."

"Yes. We call it the Milky Way Galaxy. Somewhere out near the end of one of the arms of that galaxy is a sun called Sol."

Sewall gestured toward the sky. "There is only one sun, the one that shines on us now."

Briggs persisted, "Around that sun, Sol, revolves a planet called Earth."

Sewall reached down and picked up a handful of dust from the dirt floor of the cafe. "There is one Earth, and we are on it." He shook the handful of dust under Briggs's nose. "This is Earth. You see?"

"There is another Earth, the real Earth."

"Show it to me," the scout demanded.

"You can't see it from here, not even with a telescope."

"A telescope? What's a telescope?"

Mike began angrily, "You stupid little. . . ."

Briggs stopped him. "Never mind, Mister Phillips. Our friend says there is no other Earth. Unless we can reach the Ecolog and get her help within the next two days, the energy banks of the *Corregidor* will be exhausted, and for us, too, there will be no other Earth." He turned to Sewall. "Tell me, sir, if there are no other planets or suns, what is it you see when you look up into the night sky? What is this Great Whirlpool made of?"

The scout's answer had the ring of dogmatic certainty. "Millions of bits of glowing dust."

SEWALL paid for the lunch, treating the whole squad and his own men too. It was clear he found his outlander friends amusing enough to be worth it, especially with all those tall tales of another Earth. One does not take madmen seriously, but they can be entertaining.

He glanced at the girl called Garbage. She, like the strangers, did not fit in. But her wrongness was a familiar wrongness and part of a familiar mystery, the mystery of the Ecolog. Sewall felt uneasy when he thought about the Ecolog. Just a woman in a mask! That's what his mind said, or at least the conscious part of his mind. But another, darker portion of his mind was not so sure.

GARBAGE had not joined much in the men's conversation. The sight of all those duplicates of herself in the Hall of Mummies had roused memories that were almost buried, memories of her childhood among throngs of girls who had looked almost exactly alike. Almost! That was the key word, it now seemed to her. There must be some difference, some reason why some girls ended up in the Hall of Mummies, and others lived on in the castle in the mountains.

The Ecolog

She looked around her as she walked through the crowded streets of Arbre and, for the first time, sensed a profound alien quality. These people were as different from her as the animals they rode on and used to pull their wagons. A man was ordering a woman around. Such a thing could never happen at court! And there was a woman with children tugging at her skirts. At court there were no mothers or fathers, only the Ecolog and her court and servants, both male and female. Garbage had only the vaguest idea of what was meant by mother and father, or husband and wife.

The street around her faded from her mind, though almost by instinct she continued to follow in the wake of the gruff old commodore. (The commodore would protect her. She could trust him, if no one else.)

Her consciousness was crowded with visions.

Girls, girls, girls . . . all ages, but all with the same expressions on their faces, all with the same long, blond hair.

And a balcony that looked out over the desert, a sunlit balcony where the girls played. From this balcony she had felt she could see everything in the universe. She could see, far below, the city of Arbre, for example, though at the time nobody had told her the city's name. She could see people riding on their steeds, small as insects in the distance.

Three times girls had fallen from the balcony.

It was a long, long fall.

The girls had been killed on the rocks far below.

Nobody had made much fuss about it. Nobody had put up better railings, kept better watch over the girls who remained. Nobody had really cared, and the girls had gone on playing as if nothing had happened. Garbage, too, had not paid too much attention to the accidents, but now the memory of the screams of those falling girls echoed in her memory with a fresh horror she had not felt at the time.

The falling girls blended in her mind with the corpses in that awful hall. Could one girl die again and again endlessly, yet still be alive?

She remembered the dirigible drifting overhead to moor atop the silver tower. She remembered the shouts of greeting as the Ecolog descended in an elevator, the crowd of bright-robed witty ladies and gentlemen who gathered around her, chattering, yet never actually touching her.

She remembered looking up into a polished metal mask inset with glowing jewels. Two blue eyes had looked out through slits in the mask; the coldest eyes little Garbage had ever seen. Yet she also remembered gently murmured words, "You're a beautiful thing, beautiful." The Ecolog had such a gentle, weary voice. A woman must grow weary in 300 years.

Garbage remembered the rain on the golden tiles of the dome of the palace. It did not usually rain there on the mountaintop. More often Garbage had looked down on the rainclouds as they surrounded her castle, making it seem like a ship that sailed a soft white sea. Sometimes she'd seen lightning glimmering in the cloudy ocean and birds that swam in it like the fish in her picturebook.

She remembered the men who served her like slaves.

She remembered her pet, Wunkie. It had had eight legs and three eyes and long, blue fur and had been able to curl up in her lap and go to sleep. Wunkie had been able to speak to her—in English—but had not possessed a very large vocabulary. Sometimes, though, the pet said things that sounded very wise, in a bitter sort of way.

"I am not yours. I belong to myself. If you take good care of me, you'll get real people to take care of."

Once it had said, "You and I are alike in one way; we're both easily replaced."

She remembered a baby who had been slow to learn to walk.

The Ecolog had chopped off its head with a single, quick

thwack of her jewel-handled sword. There'd been so much blood. She'd wondered how so much blood could fit in one tiny baby. The men had cleaned up the mess.

Garbage had taken the baby's death as a warning. Garbage could walk and talk, of course. She was very good at the sports the girls participated in each afternoon: good at running, jumping, fencing and playing ball, but she had not been doing well at her lessons and had failed some of the tests her tutors gave her. Like that baby, Garbage was not perfect.

And so she waited, hardly able to sleep at night, always listening for the stealthy tread of slippered feet approaching in the hall outside her bedroom; dreaming—when she did sleep—of that masked woman who would come, sword in hand, clad in rustling folds of blue nylon tricot, to put an end to one more imperfect life.

At last the footsteps came!

Garbage had looked up into that metal mask, into those dark eyeslits, looked up from her bed at that blue-draped woman looming over her in the dim room, had seen the blade slowly rise into striking position.

But then, with the quickness that comes from a thousand mental rehearsals, Garbage had slipped from under the covers and fled.

Oh, how she'd run! Men had sprinted after her, women too. But she'd been swift. A dozen times fingers had reached out to clutch her, had grazed her flesh, but always she'd evaded them, dashed down another dark hallway, up another marble staircase, through another wide doorway. And suddenly, by accident, Garbage had found a doorway and a hall she'd never known existed and had escaped from the fortress.

As she scrambled down the mountainside, they'd still followed, shouting, waving powerful flashlights.

They'd sent a machine after her. This she remembered with particular vividness. The machine, about the size and shape of her pet, had called to her in the voice of Wunkie.

"Help! Please, help me!" the thing had called.

She'd almost been fooled, but at the last possible instant had seen the nebula-light glinting on polished metal. She'd thrown a heavy boulder at it, heard the ringing clank of stone on steel, watched the machine fall and bounce and come apart, finally coming to rest far below at the foot of the cliff. The thing had one leg left that still moved feebly, and the wind brought to her the distant cry, "Help. Please, help me."

She remembered too the airships, smaller versions of the Ecolog's great dirigible. She remembered their egg-shaped gasbags dark against the nebula, their swinging searchlights, the bullets chopping into the hillside centimeters from her head that one time when they'd caught a glimpse of her. And she remembered the cave.

But now a sound brought her abruptly back to the present.

One of the small airships was passing overhead.

Instantly she sprang into a doorway and waited until it had gone.

Then she looked around. Briggs and Phillips were nowhere in sight. She'd assumed that they too would hide from the airship, but of course they hadn't. They had continued on their way, not noticing that Garbage was no longer with them.

She hurried along in the same direction. *In a moment I'll catch up.* Street merchants, beggars, prostitutes and small children passed her in the street, bumped against her, and several of them turned to look at her with surprise and curiosity.

Something about their interest worried her.

She came to a T-intersection, looked first to the right, then to the left. No sign of the commodore. She hesitated a moment, then picked a direction at random and continued onward. She considered waiting in one spot for

Briggs to find her. But she was afraid to stay in one place. People were staring at her; if she didn't keep moving they might do more than stare.

She glanced over her shoulder.

Two grubby children were following her, watching her as if she were some sort of strange animal in a zoo. *Why do they stare like that?* she wondered. *Is it because I look like those mummies?*

The thought of the mummies gave her an inspiration.

The temple was a large, impressive building, visible from all over Arbre. If she could go there at least she wouldn't be lost, and she might persuade someone to locate Briggs for her.

At the next intersection she saw the temple. It was nearer than she'd expected. She hurried toward it. Four children were following her now.

She decided to go into the temple through the side entrance, in case there was some sort of religious service in progress. That meant going through the Hall of Mummies, an idea that did not much appeal to her; but it had occurred to her she might find some clue among all her dead sisters, some explanation for the way people stared at her, why long ago they had pampered her and now seemed determined to kill her.

As she mounted the short flight of marble steps at the side of the Temple of the Ecolog, she could not help but notice the group of children had become a small crowd; some were even young men in their teens and early twenties. She stopped at the head of the stairs and looked directly at them, hoping to scare them off, shame them, or at least intimidate them a little, but they met her gaze without blinking, without lowering their gaze, without a trace of an embarrassed smile.

They stopped at the foot of the steps and peered up at her frankly, not trying to conceal their interest. Was it the heat that made her lips feel suddenly dry, made her sway with dizziness, made the faces of the children fade in and out of focus? She turned on her heel and opened the heavy, bronze door, let herself into the Hall of Mummies and closed the door behind her. Was there some way to lock the door? If there was she could not find it.

To her relief she saw that some adults lingered in the hall. Perhaps she could engage them in conversation. Then the children would go away and leave her alone.

She spoke to an old man approaching her.

"Hello. Can you help me?"

The man stopped in his tracks, eyes round, toothless mouth hanging open. "What?" he said inanely. He nervously fingered his dirty, worn tunic.

"I'm a stranger in Arbre," she went on with determination. "Could you give me some information?"

Some of the other old people nearby had begun to stare, squinting at her in the dim light. The old man said, "What kind of information?" He was backing away from her.

She gestured toward the silent figures along the walls. "These mummies. Can you tell me what they mean?"

"What they mean?" he wheezed.

"Yes."

"You know if anybody does, young lady."

Behind her the outside door opened a crack, letting in a brilliant shaft of sunlight. The children began entering, whispering and softly giggling.

"I don't know anything about. . . ." she began, but it was obvious he didn't believe her; even that he was reluctant to talk to her.

She left him and turned her attention to a fat old lady with a baby in her puffy arms.

"Hello. I'm a stranger here and—"

"What do you want?" The old woman's voice was frightened.

"I'm trying to understand the customs of this city. For instance, I see you're holding that baby rather tightly, as if it belonged to you."

"It does. This is my son. Me and my husband don't have but one child."

"Husband? I've heard that word but I don't really understand it. What's a husband?"

"A husband's a father."

"A father? Is a father a tutor or a guard or a servant? I mean, what does a father do?"

The old woman's mouth moved silently. She turned away, as if protecting the baby from some great danger.

An old gentleman with somewhat cleaner and better-mended robes stepped forward. "Perhaps I can help."

Garbage said in a rush of relief, "There's so much I don't understand. For example, you see those bodies along the wall?"

The man's voice was gentle. "I'm sorry. I don't see anything. I'm blind." His eyes were fixed and glassy.

A ragged teenage boy called, "Hey you, how come you ask so many questions?"

Another boy chimed in, "Are you as good at answering them as you are at asking them?"

Garbage stood up straight, chin out. "If you want to ask me something, go ahead."

The boy shouted, "Why ain't you dead?"

Garbage chewed on her lip, but did not answer. Was there an answer to a question like that?

Some other boys joined in, shouting. "Why ain't you dead? Why ain't you dead?"

The fat woman waved a pudgy paw at the mummies. "The other ones are!"

The gaunt old man added indignantly, "It's indecent, you walking and talking like a regular person."

"Indecent! Indecent!" came echoing voices. The crowd was growing larger. None of the faces, young or old, was friendly. Garbage stepped back a few paces. The crowd advanced, murmuring. Garbage stopped, back to the wall. Her head was level with the narrow shelf that the mummies stood on.

"You should be dead!" called someone.

"Up on the wall with the others!" someone else put in.

The circle shouted agreement.

A huge, black-bearded man shouldered his way through the crowd, grinning, saying, "Yeah, up on the wall. Like all the rest." His big fists were like knobby clubs.

The fists opened, reached for her. The people cheered.

Her slender fingers darted up and grasped the ankle of the nearest mummy. She tugged. The mummy slid off the shelf, began to fall. She swung the corpse like a club, striking the bearded man full in the face. He screamed, fell backward and scrambled away, his face full of revulsion and disgust. The whole mob retreated a few steps amid a chorus of gasps and cries.

Garbage saw an opening appear in the previously solid wall of enemies. She let go of the corpse's ankle and butted her way through the opening. To her surprise, she found herself in the clear, running toward the temple sanctuary.

She laughed with relief, though she could hear the echoing footsteps of the mob running behind her. *My sisters*, she thought. *They'll help me.*

She reached out and grasped another dead ankle.

A stiff, white carcass, its feet snatched from under it, toppled out from the wall and fell in the path of the oncoming throng. The leaders tripped over it and sprawled on their faces; the others lost time detouring around them.

She jerked yet another foot off the shelf, then another and another. Like tumbling dominoes her dead selves rained down behind her, spreading obstruction, confusion and chaos.

Still laughing, she burst through the doorway into the sanctuary, banging the heavy door open so that it swung back and crashed into the wall.

A ceremony was in progress; the pews were full of solemn worshippers.

Three hundred pairs of astonished eyes shifted their gaze from the statue to focus accusingly upon her.

As soon as Briggs noticed Garbage was missing, he insisted on doubling back to look for her. He strode along so swiftly that short-legged Sewall had to run to keep pace.

Sewall panted, "You'll never find her. She's slipped away, gone into hiding."

Briggs glared down at him. "Nonsense, sir. The girl said she would take me to the Ecolog. She will not leave me until she has kept her promise."

The little man laughed harshly. "She is from the court, Mister Briggs. The people of the court feel no obligation to keep their word to the likes of us."

They had arrived at the intersection where Briggs last remembered seeing the girl, and there they halted. Ignoring the protests of Scout Sewall, the commodore ordered his squad to attention. They were a mere seven men, not including Briggs himself and his second-in-command, Lieutenant Mike Phillips; except for the commodore, they were all unarmed. Sewall's men, who stood nearby, were well-equipped with knives and long curved scimitars.

"At ease, men," barked the commodore, sweating.

The squad stood at ease. In their makeshift rags of scavenged parachute material Briggs's troops did not look particularly impressive, nor did their frightened sunburned faces inspire much confidence. Still, they had come this far without breaking. That was something.

The commodore spoke. "We will be leaving this city before nightfall. That native girl has promised to be our guide on the last leg of our journey. We'll be traveling through completely unfamiliar country, and rather rough country, from the little I've seen of it. I don't need to remind you of the importance of a guide under such circumstances." He paused to cough and spit in the dust at his feet. The air in Arbre was very, very dry. "I'm counting on you to find her. She has probably become lost and is wandering around somewhere close by. Deploy and search the area, but be careful not to get lost yourselves. Check back here at least every ten minutes. I'll stand here as a marker." He had chosen his point well, at the center of the intersection of six streets. "You go along too," he said to Phillips.

Phillips saluted, "Aye, sir."

The squad, on command, began to spread out, calling, "Garbage! Garbage!" It was an absurd spectacle, and Briggs could not repress a smile, particularly when some of the natives laughed outright.

Sewall, however, was perfectly serious. "You lied to your men, Mister Briggs," he said softly.

"Indeed?" said Briggs.

"Yes. You told them you would be leaving this city."

"And so I will."

Sewall shook his head slowly. "No, you're staying here for the rest of your life. Of course, the length of that life is up to you."

Sewall's men were close enough to overhear this remark, and some of them seemed quite amused.

THE troops came and went.

Some reported that natives they had questioned had seen the girl, but had been unwilling to help find her or even point out the direction she'd taken. The citizens of Arbre seemed unwilling to say anything about her at all, as if she was something loathsome, frightening or taboo.

Briggs said to Sewall, "Perhaps if your men did the questioning—"

"My men have better things to do," snapped the little brown man.

"Then let me question you."

"I'm at your service."

"What's so special about this girl? Why is everyone acting so strangely toward her?"

"Strangely? No one is acting strangely except you, with your insane fantasies about other planets. It's natural to want things to be as they should be, to want the dead to lie down and be still instead of running around causing trouble among the living."

"This girl is not dead."

Sewall looked up at the Commodore with pity. "Perhaps not technically, but you saw those mummies in the temple."

"Yes."

"Didn't she look exactly like them?"

"Yes." He shrugged.

The little man was triumphant. "Then that's where she belongs, you see!"

Briggs changed his tack. "How did those girls in the temple die?"

"If you'd looked close you would have seen that some had slit throats. Most though, were stabbed through the heart, and of course you couldn't see that through their tunics. We cleaned up the blood."

"Where did they come from?"

Sewall gestured off-handedly toward the mountains. "From Abbutututikan, the palace of the Ecolog."

"Who killed them?"

"The Ecolog."

"Why?"

"I don't know. They say it's because they didn't measure up in some way, but I say it's the whim of the Ecolog. When you're the absolute ruler of everything, you don't need to give reasons for what you do."

"How did they get here?"

"The Ecolog brought them here in her airship. On one visit she may bring one dead girl, on another visit three or four. She says we're supposed to treat them with honor so we line them up in the Hall of Mummies, but everyone knows they're human garbage, no good to the Ecolog or anyone else. Your friend is like that. Even alive you can tell she's no good."

"What do you mean?"

Sewall leaned close, frowning. "Haven't you noticed?

She's not like you and me. She doesn't fit in. I take orders. So does everyone else in Arbre. So do you, I imagine. And your crew certainly takes orders from you. But that girl doesn't. If she does something, it's because she wants to, and if she doesn't want to do something, not even the threat of death will make her do it. You see what I mean?"

Briggs nodded slowly. "I think I do."

Sewall was delighted. "Someone like that's always a danger. Your friend is smart and fast on her feet and—have you noticed?—awfully strong for a little slip of a girl. That makes her all the more dangerous! If she has a chance she'll get the better of both of us, of the whole city. But the real trouble begins when there's two of them. Imagine the struggle, the fight between them for superiority, for mastery! And what if there were ten of her, or 100, or 1,000? Chaos! A universal free-for-all!"

"So she's not garbage because she's inferior," Briggs mused.

"Of course not! She's garbage because she's superior!"

THE search had been a failure.

Very few of the natives had seen the girl, and none of them knew where she had gone. Valuable time had been lost finding two of Briggs's men who had disappeared looking for her.

Briggs scowled. "We'll have to get help."

Sewall smiled smuggly. "From whom?"

"From Lord Mayor Mano, I suppose."

"I'm afraid that will be impossible. You've had your audience with the Lord Mayor for today. With luck you might get an appointment for tomorrow or the day after."

"I can't wait. By that time your fellow citizens will almost certainly have killed her, if they haven't done so already."

"Nevertheless. . . ."

Angrily Briggs turned to his men and snapped, "Attenshun!" They hurriedly straightened up their ranks. "Right face! Forward march! Hup two three four!"

The natives watched with mild curiosity as the troops filed by. Sewall and his men followed with no pretense of discipline, openly contemptuous of the outlanders. Only a madman would march in this heat!

After a few blocks Sewall ran forward to catch up. "Wait a moment!" he called, but Briggs strode grimly on. At Briggs's elbow he pleaded, "Don't make any more trouble. She's not worth it. If you'll forget about her I'll give you one of my men to act as your guide up into the mountains."

Briggs answered, "How do I know I can trust him?"

"I'll guide you myself!"

"How do I know I can trust you?"

They rounded a corner. Ahead Briggs could see the impressive building that housed the Lord Mayor's offices, and beside it the Temple of the Ecolog.

"You have no choice, Mister Briggs," insisted Sewall, trotting along. He was like a puppy yapping at the heels of a shambling bear.

"We'll see," muttered Briggs.

They entered the city's central square. It was wide, covered with paving stones and boasted an occasional statue in the style of the planet's "Golden Age." Ahead was a broad marble staircase leading up to the front entrance of the office building, and on either side of the entrance, stood a guard. Expressionlessly, the guards watched him approach. He started up the stairs. They barred the door with their spears.

"I told you," said Sewall happily.

"Have you been sent for?" demanded the guard on the left.

Wordlessly Briggs continued up the steps, his troops behind him. Sewall's men had fallen almost a block behind, and were strolling along, enjoying the antics of the foreigners.

"Are you deaf?" growled the guard on the right.

Without warning Briggs drew his claymore and, reaching the top of the stairs, chopped the heads off the spears with two vigorous sword strokes. The guards gazed open-mouthed at their suddenly useless weapons, then one of them raised the stump of his spear as if to use it as a club.

Briggs efficiently and unceremoniously kicked him in the stomach. The man dropped his spear stump and, moaning, clutched his stomach. The other guard voluntarily threw down his weapon and backed away fearfully.

Now Sewall was drawing a sword, the long curve-bladed scimitarlike type Briggs had seen so often here in Arbre. Claymore at the ready, Briggs faced him and said softly, "Do you really want to do that?"

Sewall hesitated, then slowly slipped his blade back into its scabbard. "Perhaps not, my friend." The little man's voice betrayed no emotion.

Briggs stepped around the groaning guard and entered the building.

LORD Mayor Mano sat for a moment at the radio table, pale and unhappy; then he reached out and switched off the set. Slowly, with shaking hands, he removed his headphones and laid them on the table. He pushed back his heavy, wooden chair with a rasping scrape and rose unsteadily to his feet. More gaunt and skeletal than ever, his black robes hung from his bony limbs like a shroud.

"I'm not ready," he murmured.

He squared his shoulders and stepped from behind the curtain into his office.

He seated himself in his heavy wooden chair behind the massive desk and glanced toward the window that looked out onto his balcony. Estimating the time of day from the angle of the sun, he decided it was almost suppertime. He could, if he wished, quit work now with a clear conscience, if only it weren't for. . . .

He thought of the radio message he had just received

and his hard-won composure almost collapsed. He asked himself, in an effort at self-consolation, *Can anything worse happen?*

As if in answer to his question, a startled cry came from the other side of his office door. Frowning, he half rose. There was a thud, as of a falling body; then the door burst open, or rather, was kicked open.

"What . . . ?" Lord Mayor Mano began.

Before he could say another word Commodore Abraham Briggs entered, strode swiftly to his desk, leaned over it and thrust the point of his sword within centimeters of the Lord Mayor's throat.

Briggs boomed, "No more delays, sir! You will radio the dirigible and you will do it now."

Mano shrank back in his chair. "No, I. . . ."

The commodore continued relentlessly, "You will tell the pilot to fly here at once and transport me to the Ecolog."

Mano protested, "There's no need. . . ."

Lieutenant Mike Phillips brandished the scimitar he had taken from Sewall. "That's what you think!"

The outlander's troops were now filing in, together with their shame-faced prisoners. Sewall looked particularly depressed.

Mano was slightly cross-eyed from looking at the sword point next to his throat. "You don't understand. The dirigible radioed me not more than a few minutes ago. It's on its way here to do exactly what you want."

"To take us to the Ecolog?" Briggs demanded.

The Lord Mayor nodded carefully, trying not to touch the sword. "That's right. I am to go with you. If you'll put away your weapon—"

"Not yet," said Briggs. "First you have to command your guards to go away and leave us alone."

Mano turned his head slightly. Sure enough some of Arbre's crack troops were outside the door with scimitars drawn. "Go away! Go away!" croaked the Lord Mayor. "Do you want these insane outlanders to slit my throat?"

Reluctantly the soldiers withdrew.

"Now will you lower that sword?" With disgust, Mano heard the pleading tone in his own voice.

"One more thing," said Briggs. "One of our party is missing, the girl called Garbage."

"She's not here!" said the Lord Mayor.

"I can see that, sir. But have your men killed her?"

"No, no! I swear it!"

"Have they captured her?"

"Never! I gave no such order! I have heard no such report!"

"There are some soldiers gathering in the square," warned Mike. He had taken up a position at the window.

"Good," roared Briggs turning to Mano, "Get up, sir."

As Briggs stepped back a pace, the Lord Mayor stood up, slowly and carefully.

Briggs gestured with the claymore. "Now, out on the balcony, Lord Mayor Mano. Move!"

The Lord Mayor obeyed.

The light, as he stepped out into the open air, temporarily dazzled him, but he could hear the excited murmur of the crowd below. Mano squinted, blinked. Now he could dimly make out the small crowd of soldiers and citizens milling aimlessly around in the square. He thought, *They don't know how to deal with things like this. We've been at peace too long.*

Right behind him Briggs growled, "Tell them to find the girl."

Mano shouted, "The outlanders want the garbage girl who came here with them. Can you find her?"

He heard a disgusted voice from the crowd, "We've found her already."

"Where is she?" The Lord Mayor asked, his tone feverishly eager.

"In the Temple of the Ecolog," came the answer. "The priests are holding her for sacrilege, blasphemy, vandalism and the Ecolog only knows what else."

Briggs whispered, "Tell them to bring her here."

"Bring her here," called the Lord Mayor.

A groan of disappointment arose from the crowd. A woman's voice broke through the general murmur. "She's a garbage girl! She ought to be dead, like the others!"

Briggs roared, "Do you want your Lord Mayor dead?"

A hush fell over the crowd.

"Do what they say!" blurted Mano, his voice cracking.

There was a general grumbling, but several soldiers sprinted off in the direction of the nearby temple.

Mano felt faint. Surely this was a nightmare. Things like this don't really happen.

Then he spotted the soldiers returning slowly. The temple door stood open and seven priests emerged. Between them was the girl, her hands tied behind her and a chain, like a leash, attached to a collar around her throat. One of the priests held the other end of the chain.

How frightfully slowly they descended the stairs and across the broad expanse of the square! Why must priests always be so slow? Would they preserve their dignity at the expense of a man's life?

"Tell them to free her," Briggs muttered.

"Let her go!" Mano wailed. "Let her go! Don't just stand there!"

The priests hesitated, then undid her hands and removed the collar.

Laughing and waving her hand, she broke away from her escort and ran toward the balcony. Mano heard her voice, faint and far away, yelling, "I knew they couldn't hold me!" As she approached the crowd, it parted to let her through. Mano thought, *Why doesn't someone grab her and force them to trade her for me?* No one did.

The commodore said, his tone almost friendly, "Lord Mayor, are you good at jumping?"

Mano felt ill. "No. Why do you ask?"

"Because you and I—all of us—are going to jump from this balcony to the square below. It's not far. Only one story. Less if you hang by your hands from the edge."

"Hang from the edge?" Mano was horrified.

"Mister Phillips, you jump first," the commodore commanded. "Keep our friend Mano company when he lands."

"Aye sir." Mike saluted.

"Tell the crowd to back away and make room for us," said Briggs.

In despair, Mano relayed the order, and the crowd reluctantly retreated. Garbage arrived and stood below, head back, grinning. Her hair was even more tangled than usual; her clothes were filthy and shredded; her skin was covered with cuts and bruises; but her eyes gleamed with delighted excitement.

Mike swung himself over the massive stone railing, scrambled down to hang by his fingertips from the ledge at the railing's foot, then let go and dropped quite gracefully to the pavement below. Garbage greeted him with an enthusiastic hug.

"Where's the dirigible, Mano?" asked Briggs.

"It's coming! It's coming! I swear it's coming!" cried Mano.

Briggs chuckled, then said, "All right, Lord Mayor. It's your turn to jump."

Mano pleaded. "Leave me here. I give you my word. . . ."

"Having you with us, at least until we finally meet your famous Ecolog, is better than your word," the commodore replied. "Now, over you go."

Lord Mayor Mano was dangling by his fingertips when he heard the distant, fluttering roar of the airship's propellers. He glanced over his shoulder and saw the great silver cigar-shape approaching over the rooftops, gleaming ghost-like in the afternoon light.

Then he let go and dropped with a sickening rush.

CHAPTER 7

The Ecolog was alone; she paced her throne room with long impatient strides, her voluminous blue gown swirling around her like a cloud, the slap of her sandals on the serpentine, mosaic floor echoing in the high, vast, shadowed vault of the ceiling. The room was lit by imitation torches that protruded from the walls at intervals; although the torches looked quite realistic, they were actually only methane gas jets. She cast many shadows as she strode, gaunt, grotesque demons that, in imitating her every movement, seemed to mock and deride her, to belittle and obscenely caricature her.

She was weary, yet she could not rest.

Her platinum mask was heavy, but she dared not remove it. Too many people already knew what it concealed! Her jeweled sword slapped against her thigh with every step, but she dared not take it off. At any moment she might have need of it. It seemed to her she was using it more and more every day. She did not love killing, as some in the court whispered; but so much killing had to be done, and she reserved the power of life and death to herself. Who else could be trusted with such a responsibility?

This day she'd had to kill 25 of the special girls.

Too many! Too many! Tomorrow would it be 50? One hundred? And where was the justice of it? It wasn't their fault they weren't perfect.

I must be getting old, she thought.

She drew her long, curved scimitarlike saber and lunged toward one of her shadows. Flèche! Parry the riposte! A head cut! A flank cut! There, there and there! Her blade swished and hummed as she danced forward and back. Suddenly she was laughing. *That's what I need! A worthy opponent!* A worthy opponent would bring back her youth.

Still chuckling with exhilaration, she sheathed her saber and strode toward the rear of the throne room.

She pushed open the intricately carved wooden doors and emerged onto her balcony, crossed to the railing and gazed down at the city of Arbre, so far below.

She saw the dirigible settling toward the city square.

She thought, *I wonder if they still study the ancient art of fencing on other worlds.*

It was an exciting possibility.

THEY stood in the city square, gazing up at the slowly descending dirigible; Lieutenant Mike Phillips, the girl called Garbage, the hostages—Sewall the Scout and Lord Mayor Mano—the seven ragged crewmen and Commodore Abraham Briggs.

Briggs had been the last to jump from the balcony. He now stood close to Sewall and Mano, claymore drawn, eyes occasionally darting nervously around at the crowd that encircled him. The citizens of Arbre were murmuring dangerously but had thus far made no hostile moves.

Nearby, Phillips was guarding Sewall with the little man's own saber, but Sewall was probably not an important enough man to make a good hostage. Some of the people in the crowd might decide Sewall was expendable.

The dirigible halted some distance from the ground. From its cantilevered rear deck a dozen crewmen, clad in blue tunics and black boots, swung downward on cables. Upon landing, they quickly tied their cables to some of the heavier statues in the square. The propellers were moving so slowly Briggs could clearly see the individual, paddle-shaped blades. He could also see richly robed men and women gazing down at him from the windows with expressions of mild curiosity. The only one on the ship who seemed excited was a fat man in a shimmering, iridescent robe. He was leaning so far over the thin railing of the rear deck Briggs was afraid he might fall.

Now that the ship was safely tied down, a broad panel opened in the belly of the gondola and a metal staircase telescoped out. The foot of the staircase struck the paving stones with a resounding clank and immediately a squad of crewmen armed with some sort of rifles appeared and started down the steps.

Briggs grasped the arm of the Lord Mayor and touched the blade of the claymore to the old man's throat.

"We're going to meet them," said Briggs in an undertone. "Easy now."

"Anything you say," was the frightened reply.

The crewmen fanned out at the foot of the stairs and stood to attention in two lines.

Two more men emerged from the gondola; a slender oriental and a tall, gaunt, brown-skinned fellow with dark hair. Both wore blue tunics and capes and black knee-high boots, but the taller had three white bands sewn on his short sleeves.

With Briggs and Mano in the lead, and Phillips, Sewall, Garbage and the men from the *Corregidor* close behind, the commodore's party moved cautiously toward the stairs.

At the foot of the steps the tall man straightened and gave Briggs a crisp salute, heels coming together with an audible click. "Captain Klain, second-in-command to the Ecolog, supreme ruler of the environment and all it contains, at your service, sir."

Briggs would have liked to return the salute, but he could not do it without losing his grip on Lord Mayor Mano. He contented himself with saying awkwardly, "I'm Commodore Abraham Briggs of the starship *Corregidor*."

Klain replied, "Please accept my profoundest apologies for my delay in contacting you. My only wish now is that you will permit me to take you to Her Royal Majesty, the Ecolog, and allow her to attempt to make amends to you all."

Briggs said, "It's too late for one of us."

Klain paled and fell silent for a moment. Then he said,

"I know. Damn it, Commodore, I'd give anything. . . ."

"Never mind," said Briggs, impressed by Klain's apparent sincerity.

Klain gestured toward the claymore. "If you'll put away your sword—"

"Not yet."

Klain frowned. "Her Majesty will not be pleased if you arrive at court with such a hostile attitude."

"Her Majesty has only herself to blame for my attitude. May we come aboard?"

Klain hesitated, then nodded. "All right." He stood aside.

Briggs, still keeping a firm grip on his claymore and his hostage, started up the steps, the rest of his little band following closely.

At the head of the stairs he passed a young woman with a rumpled white shift and a look of bruised resentment. She was close enough for him to smell the strong aroma of alcohol on her breath.

Inside the gondola a crowd of robed men and women were milling about, murmuring to each other, occasionally giggling. Many of them had drinks in their hands. Glancing around, Briggs realized he was in a cocktail lounge. No one ventured to speak to him. An uncomfortable silence developed, broken only by the muted clink of glasses, the muttering of the onlookers, and the swish-swish of the slow-turning propellers. Somewhere soft music was playing. The floor was moving ever so slightly, like the floor of a boat.

It was mercifully cool and dim. The dirigible was obviously air-conditioned. Briggs realized that he was dirty and sticky with sweat, while his audience was perfectly clean and dry. He smelled bad, too, though until now he had not been aware of it. No wonder they were whispering and staring.

He licked his cracked, dry lips and suddenly felt infinitely weary. The hundred little pains he had successfully ignored up to now suddenly intruded onto his conscious-ness. He closed his eyes and swayed.

"Careful!" cried Mano in alarm. The sword had pricked his neck.

Briggs dragged himself alert, feeling very old.

Phillips and Sewall stood close by. Phillips said, "Are you all right, Commodore?" His voice was low and worried.

"Yes, I think so."

Then Briggs noticed that he was not the focus of the crowd's attention after all. It was Garbage they were star-ing at; it was she they were whispering about.

Unafraid, she glared at them. Briggs realized she had changed. No trace of the hysterical waif who'd cringed at the sight of the *Manta* shuttlecraft remained; under all the dirt, this was a new, strange young woman, whose eyes gleamed with an intense excitement that was kin to mad-ness. Her whole bearing seemed to say, "Now it's the world's turn to be afraid of *me*!"

Briggs heard Klain ask, "Wing, is everyone on board?"

The man answered, "Yes, sir."

"Retract the ladder," said Klain.

"Yes, sir."

An electric motor hummed; clanking and rattling, the ladder was withdrawn into the hull. The panel in the floor slid shut. All these things Briggs heard rather than saw. There were people between him and the machinery, and his vision had, for some reason, become blurred.

I've got to hang on a little bit longer, he thought through the dizziness.

Klain was giving commands, listening to shouted an-swers. Dimly Briggs understood that the cables were being untied, that the ship was being freed.

Klain was speaking into an intercom. "Take her up, Nord."

"Yes, sir," crackled the intercom.

And now crewmen, who had come hand-over-hand up

the cables, were scrambling onto the rear deck. Briggs could hear them shouting cheerfully to each other.

The swish-swish of the propellers turned into a roar. The floor tilted slightly. All the lovely sophisticated people in the lounge stood quietly, but Briggs was almost thrown off balance.

The fat man in the shimmering robe pushed through the throng. Grinning broadly, he extended his puffy hand. "Welcome, offworlder. My name is Omen."

"Get back," Briggs warned. "Or your Lord Mayor's a dead man."

Omen paused, annoyed. "Are you threatening me?"

"Get back," Briggs repeated thickly. "Or I'll kill him."

Omen sighed. "He's about due for retirement anyway."

A ripple of laughter went through the crowd.

"Get back I say," said Briggs. For an instant his eyes failed to focus.

Omen moved with amazing suddenness. In a single deft movement he drew a heavy-bladed knife from the ample sleeve of his robe and threw it, backhand. The Lord Mayor uttered a single, strangled cry, before falling forward, the knife buried in his throat, his face contorted with an expression of terror and surprise.

The Lord Mayor sprawled, face down and spread-eagled on the thick, rich carpet. The crowd was silent. Briggs stared stupidly at the corpse as the floor tilted again and forced him to struggle to retain his balance.

Mike said, "We still have Sewall." His voice lacked conviction.

"And I," said Omen, "have another knife." With leering satisfaction the fat man drew it slowly from his other sleeve.

Sewall said quietly, "Outlander, do you think he cares if I live or die?"

"I suppose not," said Mike, lowering his sword.

Briggs, claymore in hand, stood unsteadily in the center of an open area. The riflemen, he saw, were filing in, raising their guns. The civilians were drawing back to get out of the line of fire.

Captain Klain stepped forward. "Drop your weapons, Outlanders."

Briggs looked at the guns, then at the corpse on the floor. Slowly, he opened his hand. The claymore dropped to the floor with a muffled clunk.

Mike Phillips followed his example.

With a cry of delight, Sewall snatched up his saber and flourished it exultantly. "My darling, my baby! You've come back to me!"

Omen stood thoughtfully, weighing his knife in his bloated fingers, testing its balance. "Klain?" he prompted.

"Commodore Briggs," said Captain Klain, "will you do me the honor of accompanying me to the cockpit?"

The commodore's voice was a painful, unnatural croak. "Why, thank you, sir. I believe I will—" he paused, shuffled to one side as the airship shifted again "—accept your kind invitation."

He fell against a table, almost overturned it, then staggered toward the waiting Klain.

Smiling, Omen followed.

BRIGGS sat like a rag doll, strapped into the navigator's chair. Captain Klain, occupying the copilot's seat, half turned to face the commodore. The doorway leading into the radio compartment was filled with the broad, robed body of Omen who, unable to wedge into any of the chairs, contented himself with dangling from a hangstrap and leaning against the doorjamb.

Through the window in the floor Briggs could see the heavily wooded foothills of the mountain range passing below, tinged crimson by the light of the setting sun.

The propellers had settled into a steady drone; the dirigible was tilted nose-up, gaining altitude.

"Water, Commodore?" Klain asked gently.

"Yes." Briggs nodded slowly.

Klain poured him a glass of water from the pilot's canister and handed it to him.

Briggs was careful not to drink too much too fast.

"I don't know what got into me," said Briggs, his voice stronger.

"Sometimes," said Klain, "the change from the hot outside to the cool inside is a shock to the system. Are you feeling better?"

"I think I'll be all right now." Briggs was surprised by the tall stranger's concern, and found himself liking him against his better judgment. There was one thing, however, he had to ask. "Old Mano . . . did you have to kill him?"

Klain glanced angrily at Omen, saying, "That's a good question."

Omen said defensively, "We didn't have time for anything else."

Briggs was puzzled. "Time?"

Omen said, "And we don't have time for a lot of explanations, either."

Klain was flustered. "I know, I know. In half an hour we'll be in Abbutututikan. Before that we must make you see. . . ." He hesitated, searching for the right words.

Omen broke in. "We have to make you see how we can be useful to you."

Klain said, "You know what our planet is like. It's slowly sliding into a sort of new Dark Age. Do you understand?"

"I understand. I think I understood almost from the beginning, except for the details."

Klain leaned forward eagerly. "Then you see how we need you, how we need fresh contacts with the rest of humanity, with other planets, other peoples. Out where you come from I'm sure mankind has progressed far beyond anything we could imagine here in this stagnant backwater. You can give us new technology, new theories, and new. . . ."

Omen prompted, "Never mind about that. Tell him what *we* can do for *him*."

"What Omen is trying to say is that we want to join with you, to help you conquer this planet," said Klain.

This is something I didn't expect. Aloud, Briggs said, "I don't want to conquer this planet."

Omen was indignant. "Of course you do!"

Briggs shook his tired head. "No, I don't."

The fat man began to sweat. "If you didn't come here to conquer, what did you come here for?"

"It was an accident."

Omen extended a shaking finger. "Don't try to lie to me. You must have come here for something. There must be something you want."

Briggs considered a moment. "Well, there *is* something."

The fat man's eagerness was pitiful. "Tell me! What is it? Ask for anything! Anything at all!"

"Do you suppose," said Briggs blandly, "you could loan me a little computer time?"

After a moment's silence, Omen said, "Is that all?"

"That's all."

Omen was suddenly all smiles. "Of course! Of course we'll loan you all the computer time you want, after we have seized power."

"I don't see why you have to seize power before I can have my computer time," said Briggs reasonably. "The Ecolog will give me the time I need."

Klain and Omen looked at each other helplessly.

Then Omen's hand dipped into his sleeve and reappeared holding a heavy-bladed knife. "Care to reconsider?" he purred.

"You won't use that on me," said Briggs.

"Why not?" said Omen.

"Because the Ecolog wouldn't like it. I assume that since you have not yet pulled off your little coup, the Ecolog must have ordered you to bring me to her."

Their faces told Briggs he was right.

"Don't worry," he went on, "I won't tell her about your plots and schemes. That's none of my business."

Klain looked up at Omen with exasperation. "All right, Omen. What do we do now?"

Omen returned his knife to his sleeve, saying smoothly, "We take the outlanders to the Ecolog, of course."

Klain was desperate. "But she'll win Briggs over!"

Omen smiled. "I'm sure she will. She'll win him over . . . to our side."

WHEN Briggs emerged from the forward compartments she was waiting for him. Everyone else on the ship hung back, perhaps from fear, perhaps from snobbery, but as if she were an old friend, Mara had come forward and asked, "Did you join them?"

He'd said no.

She'd said, "I'm glad. They want to hurt the Ecolog."

Now she stood among them, speaking to Mike Phillips, the *Corregidor* crewmen, and even the girl called Garbage, with that easy friendliness that alcohol sometimes makes possible between strangers.

In the last rays of the setting sun, the face of the mountain glowed red. The fortress of Abbututikan, too, and the golden-domed palace shone crimson in the fading light. Through the floor-to-ceiling windows in the lounge, Briggs could see the massive shapes of a semicircle of dirigible hangers almost lost in shadow and, farther down the other side of the mountain, tier on tier of immense boxlike windowless buildings.

"What are those, Mara?" Briggs asked, pointing.

"Factories," she answered softly.

"I see, and where do the workers live?"

She looked at him with surprise. "There are no workers. The factories are fully automated. They're the only factories on Earth."

This expression struck Briggs as odd. "On Earth?"

"Of course. This is Earth. That's the name of our planet."

He understood what he had only suspected before; that this planet had no name of its own, but was called Earth by those who lived here. He'd seen it happen before. Scattered through the human stellar empire were hundreds of planets named simply "Earth."

A broad-wingspanned, native bird soared in close to stare at them through the window. The passengers could glimpse its teeth and third eye. As it banked away, Garbage said, "What's that? I've never seen anything like it."

Mara said lightly, "I don't know what it's called, but we've been seeing a lot of them lately."

Garbage frowned and said to Briggs, "We used to think native creatures could survive only after we'd performed operations on their lungs. Our pets and steeds and beasts of burden all have had operations."

Briggs said, "Nature—or blind chance—performs a different sort of operation. It's frightfully wasteful, but permanent. A thousand, a million, individuals die when an environment changes, but in some species a few always somehow survive and breed."

Garbage looked at him with an odd expression. "And the survivors are superior, aren't they?"

Briggs said, "Until the environment changes again."

Other birds were visible now, but they were too far away for Briggs to make out any details. They, too, were probably native. He had not yet seen a single creature on this "Earth" that could trace its ancestry to another planet. This was not one of those planets visited by a "space ark" full of terrestrial flora and fauna in deep freeze. Perhaps that was why the terraforming was relapsing in spite of the Earth-normal, artificially formed atmosphere.

The desert was in darkness, as were the foothills and the first range of mountains. Only this mountain peak continued to be bathed in bloody light. In the palace shadowy figures were silhouetted in freshly illuminated windows as the dirigible came alongside the dome.

The propellers slowed, reversed pitch, speeded up again. The airship stopped over the courtyard and hovered.

Briggs could hear the crewmen climbing over the side, swinging downward on their mooring cables. The airship settled slowly. The propeller roar faded into a swish-swish. There was a slight jerk as one of the cables connecting the airship to snubbing posts on the ground pulled taut. The motors died altogether and the paddle-shaped blades ceased turning. In the sudden silence distant voices could be heard shouting commands, and the faint creaks and sighs of the flexing gasbag became audible.

Briggs said to Garbage, "Stay close to us."

She answered softly, "I'm no fool."

They headed toward the landing stairs, where crewmen were now standing ready and passengers were lining up to disembark. Klain and Omen appeared.

"Here comes trouble," said Mike in a low voice.

Klain approached.

"Captain Klain," said Briggs. "I hope you can arrange an interview with the Ecolog as soon as possible." He thought, *Tomorrow or never.* At about this time tomorrow night, the energy banks of the *Corregidor* would be empty.

Klain answered, "The Ecolog will see you in her own good time. I can do nothing until I have independent authority. If you are considering betraying us, remember that we may turn out to be your only hope of getting what you want." This was said in a low, nervous voice. Klain was obviously under stress.

"I realize that," answered Briggs.

Klain turned and called out, "Lower the stairs!"

BRIGGS realized several things about the threatened palace revolution. First, the conspirators were gambling on help from offworld. Second, if it succeeded, they would still obtain the offworld help they wanted, since they would be the power the offworlders must deal with. *As I feared, my mere presence here may be enough to destroy their civilization.*

He stood at the head of the stairs, gazing down into the gathering shadows. At the foot of the stairs two files of troops in blue tunics lined an aisle that the visitors would be expected to pass through. The troops were armed with rifles. They were honor guards, but guards nonetheless.

"Take my arm, Garbage," whispered Briggs.

She obeyed. Together they started slowly down the stairs, Phillips, Mara and the *Corregidor* crewmen following. The other passengers had already disembarked and now stood behind the lines of soldiers, watching Briggs.

At the far end of the aisle of soldiers stood two long-robed women, silhouetted against a tall, open doorway leading into the brightly lit interior of the palace.

"Who are they?" Briggs asked Garbage softly.

"Marcia, of the House of Green, and Angora, one of the supervisors for the tutors."

"What's the House of Green?"

"An order of nobility in the court for noblewomen."

"And noblemen?"

"There are no noblemen."

"I might have known." Briggs chuckled.

Klain met them at the foot of the steps and fell into step beside them as they proceeded between the two files of soldiers. At their approach to Marcia of the House of Green and the supervisor Angora, Klain saluted smartly and said, "My ladies, allow me to present Commodore Abraham Briggs of the starship *Corregidor.*"

Marcia of Green stepped forward, smiling. Her robes were the color of her order and she appeared to be wearing emerald rings, bracelets, necklaces and earrings. She was in her forties, but exercise, diet and tasteful makeup had preserved, it seemed, her slimness, her health and youthful appearance. Only at close range did the lines of care and responsibility in her face betray her true age.

"Welcome to Earth, Commodore. I am Marcia of Green." Her voice was cultured, soft, yet rich and reverberant, like the voice of a trained singer. She extended her hand, and Briggs gallantly kissed it.

Her companion stepped forward, and was introduced by Marcia.

Angora was also in her forties. She was dressed in black robes without jewelry or makeup, yet she too was slim and attractive. She was well named: there was more than a suggestion of the cat in her graceful movements and her green, slightly slanted eyes.

Angora did not offer a hand to be kissed but only said, "I'm here to see to the needs of your friend." She gestured toward Garbage.

Garbage clutched Briggs's arm, hard.

Briggs said smoothly, "I'd rather she stayed with me, if you don't mind."

Angora drew herself up stiffly. "She's one of the special girls. I'm responsible for her."

Briggs's voice was firm. "She stays with me."

Klain broke in diplomatically, "Forgive him, Lady Angora. He is unfamiliar with our customs."

"It's time he learned!" said Angora sharply.

Marcia said, "Never mind, Angora. It isn't worth making a scene."

A look of pure hatred passed between the two courtly ladies, and Angora said, "As you wish, my dear." She stepped back with a curtsy.

Marcia of Green, a note of petty triumph in her voice, invited "Won't you come in? It must have been a long hard journey if, as I've been told, you've come all the way from another planet."

Briggs answered, "Yes, it's been quite a trip, but the last few days have been the hardest."

As they entered the palace, Garbage whispered, "You may not know it, but you just saved my life."

"I gathered as much," said the commodore.

The Ecolog

The entrance hall had a high ceiling—at least three stories high—and an echo. The walls were decorated with brilliant, jewellike murals in the style Briggs had come to recognize as belonging to this civilization's "Golden Age." Geometry, perspective, anatomy and color combined in a display of sheer virtuosity unequaled since the days of Dante Gabriel Rossetti and Sir Lawrence Alma-Tadema. The central panel, located above the entrance doorway, was a painting of the Ecolog, arms extended, her right side brightly lit and her left in shadow. In her right hand she held a loaf of bread; in her left a human skull. The metal mask was almost transparent, so Briggs could see the barest suggestion of the face behind it. The other murals portrayed all the people of the planet at their various occupations. Each person was looking toward the Ecolog. The total effect was breathtaking.

Such art, Briggs mused, leads the beginning student to despair or, at least, rebellion.

Halfway down the hall, in the center of the mosaic floor, stood what appeared to be an immense crystal ball. As he neared it, Briggs realized it was a huge holographic image of the Milky Way Galaxy.

"Lady Marcia, could you wait a moment?" said Briggs. The procession halted.

"What is it?" inquired Lady Marcia politely.

Briggs gestured toward the sphere. "Can you show me where we're located on that—er—map?"

"Certainly." She stepped to the base of the sphere and moved her hand over some studs.

Studs, not switches, thought Briggs. *High technology.*

An arrow appeared in the holograph.

"There," said Lady Marcia.

"As I expected," said Briggs with satisfaction.

The arrow pointed to a star that was part of a globular cluster in what was called the halo of the galaxy. It was slightly below the plane of the spiral arms and three-quarters of the way out from the bulbous nucleus at the hub, a good deal closer in than the two Magellanic Clouds.

Turning, Briggs noticed that Sewall the scout was staring at the image with stunned incredulity. There were other planets and other suns after all, not just dust motes in the sky!

Returning his attention to the globe, Briggs easily located the white giants, Altair and Sirius. Somewhere between them, he knew, was his own solar system. There was no doubt in his mind now that he could find his way home, if only he had the fuel for the trip.

"Thank you," he said with a nod to Lady Marcia. "That was very interesting. And now could we talk to the Ecolog?"

Lady Marcia answered quietly. "No, I'm afraid not. You'll have to wait." She turned and began walking away from the sphere. "Follow me, please."

Briggs said. "It's important that I speak to her at once!" He walked briskly after her.

"That's quite impossible," she said.

"Then can I speak to the head of your computer department?"

"Not without the Ecolog's permission."

"May I contact my starship?"

"No, not unless the Ecolog authorizes the communication."

"We are the Ecolog's guests. We deserve some consideration!"

Marcia smiled politely. "You think so?"

Out of the corner of his eye Briggs saw Captain Klain. The captain seemed amused by some private joke.

Marcia was leading them into a small room near the end of the hall. "You will wait here," she said.

Briggs glanced around. Comfortable-looking, black, imitation-leather chairs and couches were placed about the room, as well as a large television set with a two-meter-square screen. Mike, Garbage, and, surprisingly, Mara settled into one cluster of chairs, the seven crewmen from the *Corregidor* into another.

"What are we supposed to do while we wait?" asked Mike.

"You can watch televison," said Lady Marcia. "The fights are on tonight, on closed circuit."

"The fights?" asked one of the crewmen hopefully.

"The insect fights." Lady Marcia turned on the set. "We have a studio in the basement, with a magnifying lens on the camera. "You'll be surprised to see some insects from your home planet, carefully bred for generations from a few stowaways found on the ship we arrived in 300 years ago."

Music began to play. Briggs recognized the "Thunder and Blazes March." An announcer was in the middle of his spiel. "And in this corner we have Hairy Harry the Tarantula, champion for three weeks running. Tough little rascal; isn't he?" There was a chorus of female boos. As the picture came into focus, Briggs was dismayed to see, three-dimensional and in color, a monstrous hairy spider inching along.

The announcer continued, "Harry is all ready to tangle, in mortal combat, with game little Battlin' Bessie the Wasp. And here she is now!"

There was a high-pitched whining buzz and the camera was raised to reveal a small wasp flying in quick angry circles above the tarantula. Again, they could hear a chorus of feminine cheers, mingled with a few masculine boos. The announcer's voice rose with excitement. "Bess is making her first pass!"

From the doorway, Klain called, "Enjoy yourselves."

Klain, Sewall, Marcia and Angora strolled away gossiping, leaving behind a troop of riflemen to stand guard.

The announcer was saying, "He missed her! She's circling again. This is a big night, ladies and gentlemen. After this fight don't miss the big event! Yes, I kid you not! It's

big-time team excitement with the ants versus the termites!
And now Battlin' Bess is making her second pass!"

Briggs heard one of his crewmen shout, "Go get 'um,
Bess!"

THE Great Whirlpool was bright; when one is even slightly
above the plane of the galaxy, an incredible number of
stars are visible—ones that are hidden from the inhabitants
of the solar system and its neighbors by a disk of dust. The
gleaming, moonlike snowball of stars at the center was
quite plain; even the dimmer, curving bands of the spiral
arms on the opposite side, could be seen, although they
were distorted by perspective.

Captain Klain stood in a mountaintop garden. The air
was clear and thin, without the obscuring haze that, at
lower altitudes, sometimes blurred the sky. He had always
enjoyed standing alone like this, looking up at the heavenly
display; but now each band, each point of light took on a
new significance. He had always known there were people
out there, but it had never been quite real to him, had
never seemed to have any bearing on the affairs of his busy
life. Emotionally he'd been almost like those ignorant people who believed nothing was out in space but a lot of
shining dust motes.

Now all that was changed.

One might say the sky had fallen. At least a bit of the
sky had fallen and had intruded itself into the order of his
world. The outlanders were here! Commodore Briggs was
here! And Briggs brought with him opportunity and danger. Briggs was the spark to ignite a blaze that could not
be extinguished until it had utterly destroyed the fragile
structure the Ecolog had built here. Briggs could break
the three centuries of isolation that had brought Klain's
civilization to the brink of a new Dark Age. Briggs could
save this world or kill it!

Yet it seemed to Klain that Briggs did not understand
this or, if he understood, did not care.

Klain sighed and watched his breath condense into a steamy cloud. He shivered in the night chill. Nights, at this altitude, were always cold. He gathered his cloak about his body and looked impatiently in the direction of the palace. Where was Omen? Omen had promised to be here half an hour ago. Had the fat man made a slip, been captured? Was he, at this moment, revealing Klain's name to the Ecolog's torturers?

Klain sat down on a large rock. A vision of the Ecolog appeared in his mind, and he felt a pain in his chest, a constriction in his throat. This woman, who must be killed, was probably the most remarkable person the human race had yet produced. He murmured to himself, "Whatever she did, she did it for us all."

He heard footsteps and glanced up sharply.

Omen, puffing and wheezing, was lumbering toward him out of the gloom.

"Klain?"

"I'm right here."

"Ah, good. I have news." The fat man settled himself on a nearby boulder to catch his breath. "Your friends Nord and Wing have joined us, and that little brown fellow, Sewall the scout."

Klain was uneasy. "Are you sure it's wise to have so many in on the plan?"

"After the assassination there may be some fighting. We'll need all the help we can get. There's something else, too." He thrust a fat hand into his cloak and produced a small, compact pistol-like weapon. "Sewall gave us a present."

Klain took it and examined it with a puzzled frown. "This is no ordinary gun. Where did he get it?"

"He took it from the offworlders when he captured them. He was supposed to hand it over to the Lord Mayor, but he kept it for his own purposes."

"Really? Then why is he giving it to us?"

Omen chuckled. "He wouldn't admit it, but I think he can't figure out how it works."

"He may not be the only one. Look how tiny the hole is at the end of the barrel. Is it some kind of ray gun? No, no, I don't think so." Klain turned it over in his hands, inspecting it as carefully as the nebula light permitted. "Ah, I see! There's a bullet clip in the handle." He snapped it loose and pulled it out.

Omen leaned close. "They're too small to be bullets." The clip was filled with what appeared to be 50 miniature rockets.

Klain snapped the clip back into the handle. "Nothing to do but fire it and see what happens."

"No, no! It might explode. . . ."

"I don't think so." Klain aimed the gun into the air and pulled the trigger.

There was a high-pitched, muffled snick and a hairline of flame was traced for an instant from the gunbarrel to the distant darkness.

"What was that?" said Omen, a little frightened.

"A self-propelled dart, or maybe you could call it a miniaturized rocket missile. It probably carries poison and I wouldn't be surprised if it had a homing device to guide it to the victim's body heat."

"How do you know all that?"

"I've seen weapons like this."

"Where?"

"In the Royal Museum." Klain slipped the offworlder pistol into his belt.

Omen said thoughtfully, "It's so small, so silent, yet so deadly . . . perfect for an assassination."

With anguish Klain saw a flash in his mind of the Ecolog falling to the floor. A quick-acting poison would not even give her time to cry out. His voice shook. "Yes, I . . . I know."

Omen smiled broadly. "The gods of history are with us,

my friend. This weapon falling into our hands is a sign."

Klain said scornfully, "Gods of history? You told me you weren't superstitious."

"It's no more than a figure of speech, my friend. Now all that remains is to decide on the moment to strike!" He slapped his hand on his knee. "The sooner the better."

Klain said, "Don't be in such a hurry. If I know the Ecolog she'll keep Briggs waiting for days ، . . on principle. The longer he waits the more likely he is to come over to our side. With his support our position will be much stronger."

Omen nodded. "A good point. Ah, the Ecolog's not as clever as everyone thinks. Look how she's playing into our hands!"

Suddenly the men were startled by the sound of running footsteps from the direction of the palace. Klain's hand flew to the offworlder pistol in his belt.

Omen raised his hand. "No, don't shoot. It's Sewall."

The little scout stumbled up to them, so out of breath he couldn't speak. Sewall wasn't at all used to the thin air at this altitude.

Omen jumped up. "What is it? What's wrong? Tell us, damn you!"

At last Sewall croaked out, "The Ecolog has . ،. granted Briggs . . . an audience."

Klain too leaped to his feet. "When? Tomorrow?"

Sewall paused, seeming to take a perverse satisfaction in the effect his words were having. "No. Tonight. Now."

BRIGGS trudged wearily along the endless passageway, his face alternately in light and shadow as he passed one after another of the simulated torches set in the walls. He had eaten, rested a little, and changed to fresh clothing brought to him by one of the Ecolog's manservants. (She did not appear to have any womanservants.) He now looked rather like one of the Ecolog's soldiers, with his blue tunic and tall black boots. From his own uniform he retained only his fingerwatch and spun-steel pocketbelt. After a moment's inner debate, he had even abandoned his dented helmet, so his almost bald head gleamed, unprotected, in the flickering torchlight.

On his right strode Lady Marcia of Green; on his left, Angora.

Mara had filled him in on all the latest gossip of the court, so he knew a great deal about these two ladies. Lady Marcia and Angora were rivals for the affection of a certain techman far below their stations; Angora sometimes drank too much; Lady Marcia was a food fadist. Briggs wondered if this information would ever do him any good. Probably not.

Lady Marcia said, "We've passed your requests on to the Ecolog."

Angora added, "She seems to be taking quite an interest in you." She favored him with an arch smile.

"If she's a reasonable woman," said Briggs, "I'm sure she'll grant my requests."

Lady Marcia's voice was mocking. "You may be in for a surprise, Commodore."

"Yes," said Angora. "Her Majesty was not happy to hear you had cost her the life of Lord Mayor Mano."

He was indignant. "I didn't kill him."

"You caused him to be killed," said Lady Marcia. "Do you think a high councillor could compromise his dignity by giving in to your threats? Omen had no choice."

"The Ecolog does not condone actions that cause her to lose her loyal citizens," said Angora.

"Her actions caused me to lose one of my men, too," Briggs said.

Lady Marcia lowered her voice. "If she was your prisoner, you could bring that up. Since you are hers, you'd be wise to be silent about it."

"Well," said Angora cheerily, "Here we are!"

The trio halted before some heavy, beautifully carved wooden doors. Lady Marcia thumped a heavy, iron knocker. The echo of the thumps had hardly died away before Briggs heard footsteps approaching on the other side of the door.

"Good luck, offworlder," said Angora a little too sweetly.

The doors swung open. A powerfully built woman soldier peered out. She carried a rifle and wore a heavy curved knife; her uniform was similar to that of the Ecolog's male soldiers—a blue tunic with tall black boots. "Follow me," she commanded.

Briggs did as he was told and, passing through the doorway, found himself in an immense, dimly lit circular hall. Ahead lay a broad marble staircase. Briggs heard the hinges squeak; then the doors shut with an echoing boom. He glanced behind to notice that Lady Marcia and Angora had remained outside.

Without another word the woman soldier led Briggs up the stairs. When they reached the top she turned to him and said in a hushed voice, "Go right in. The Ecolog is expecting you."

As the soldier stood back Briggs pushed open another heavy door much like the first, but larger. A strange aroma drifted out that Briggs recognized instantly. It was the overpowering decaying-roses smell of the ngaas.

He hesitated.

"Are you afraid?" demanded the woman soldier with contempt.

"Of course I am. I'm not an idiot!"

Nevertheless he drew himself up and stepped through the doorway. The soldier slammed the door behind him and locked it. Briggs thought, *She doesn't seem to be afraid I'll do something rash, like kidnap the Ecolog.* That, in itself, was somewhat disturbing.

He stepped cautiously forward into the shadowy room, glancing nervously around, searching for the ngaas his sense of smell told him were here.

It was a large chamber with a high ceiling, an intricate,

serpentine mosaic floor, and imitation torches protruding
from the walls to cast a ruddy dancing light over everything. There were many shadows, shadows in which almost anything might be hiding.

As he approached the center of the floor, he saw, to his
right, an alcove that had been invisible from the entrance.
There, almost motionless, crouched a huge ngaa, as big as
a greyhound, its brown, bony armor glistening as if polished, its small, disturbingly human fingers slowly flexing
open and closed. The creature was watching Briggs through
a pair of half-closed yellow eyes with cold, unwinking
indifference.

A terrible suspicion washed over him. Perhaps the
Ecolog was not here. Perhaps no one was waiting for him
but this one hungry beast.

He took a careful step backward.

A peal of rich contralto laughter echoed through the
room. Briggs stopped retreating. The ngaa was still watching him, but had made no hostile moves.

Briggs moved forward, at the same time describing a
wide circle around the alcove. A low platform came into
view, with a short flight of steps leading up to it. On the
platform was a massive carved chair decorated with glittering jewels; a throne. On the throne sat the Ecolog.

"Don't be frightened, Commodore Briggs," she said in
a low melodious voice. "He's my pet."

She was smaller than he'd expected; more like a little
girl than a goddess. Her slender body was firm and well
muscled, though her skin was pale, and her blond hair was
long and tied back in an incongruous ponytail. She lounged
more than sat, without a trace of regal dignity. The platinum mask inset with jewels and carved in curving semi-
geometrical patterns concealed her face. Was she an
impostor?

"Are you the Ecolog?" he inquired doubtfully.

She stared at him a moment through the slanting slits
in her mask; then, slowly, she began to move. First she

sat up, then hesitated. Something was happening to her. A simple change in posture had transformed her into a different woman, a woman with a stage presence, a personal magnetism that might have belonged to an Isodora Duncan, a Sarah Bernhardt, an Eleonora Duse. This uncanny transformation was, somehow, more frightening by far than the sight of her pet.

"Yes, I am," was the soft answer.

He believed her.

She was sitting now with the stillness of a dead woman, an unnatural, impossible stillness. Her voluminous blue gown settled around her like smoke, like spiderwebs. The jewels in her mask flickered, reflecting the light from the torches. There he saw a glint of red, there a glint of green, there one of blue and one of the shifting rainbow hues of diamonds or cut crystal. Hanging negligently from her belt was a curved saber in a richly decorated scabbard. The pommel, too, glinted with jewels.

Slowly, slowly, her hand began to move, though the rest of her body remained motionless. Now the arm was moving too, lifting. He watched it as a chimpanzee watches a cobra. The fingers in the hand began to move too, as if each was a separate creature. He realized, with a start, that she was beckoning him to come closer.

He shuffled forward to the base of the short flight of steps leading up to her throne.

"Sit down, Commodore," she said, indicating the steps.

I will not sit at her feet, he thought.

"No, thank you," he said stiffly. "I'd rather stand." He had already noticed that the Ecolog's throne was the only chair in sight.

"You've come a long way. You must be tired."

"I'll be all right," he said stubbornly.

The ngaa stirred, shifting its position. On closer inspection the creature's body made a kind of sense. Its rear four feet bore huge, powerful claws. It was only the front two that were like human hands. The ngaa was not so much a wolf or a spider as a grotesque travesty of a centaur.

The thing sighed, lowered its head and closed its eyes.

"As you wish," she said. "Now what was it you wanted to ask me?"

Briggs opened his mouth, but nothing came out. He had completely forgotten.

She laughed gently. "Never mind. Marcia of Green repeated to me the questions you asked her. First, you wished to speak to me. Well, as you see I've already granted that request. Second, you wished to talk to the head of the computer department. I am the head of the computer department, so your second wish is also granted. Third, you wished my permission to contact your orbiting starship. That, too, you may do. You see how foolish you were to be afraid of me? I've given you everything you wanted."

Briggs licked his dry lips. "Thank you, Your Highness, but there's more."

"Don't be greedy," she cautioned him playfully.

"I need to use your master computer."

"The answer is no." Without warning the playfulness had been replaced by a grim coldness.

A long, tense silence followed until she added, "I have answered your questions. Now you must answer one of mine. I noticed among the weapons taken from you and placed in my private armory a sword. Tell me, Commodore, do you fence?"

He answered cautiously, "A little."

"When you are rested you must give me the pleasure of a duel. In a few days—"

"I don't have a few days."

"Ah, but you are mistaken. Here you are and here you shall stay." She relaxed somewhat, sitting back in her throne, once again human. "You were not invited to Abbututtutikan. You forced yourself upon us. Therefore you owe us at least a bit of entertainment to pay for your room and board."

"Entertainment?" said Briggs with dismay.

"It's not much to ask in return for the life of the Lord Mayor of Arbre. Not much to ask in return for the damage that garbage girl you harbor has done in my temple. Not much to ask for the shock your presence here has caused to my people. It is not healthy for them to be set dreaming of other worlds and galactic empires, of vast corrupt bureaucracies, of life-styles drowning in waste and pollution, of scientific miracles that end in disaster and philosophical ideas that make people restless, unhappy and violent. It was to escape all these evils that we came here. It was to remain free of them that we separated ourselves from the rest of mankind for 300 years."

. He broke in desperately. "There are things you don't know about—"

"I'm sure there are many things out where you've come from I don't know about. Would it make me happy to know about wars between star systems? Would it make me happy to know about weapons of genocidal magnitude? Would it make me happy to know about the crime, sickness, injustice and natural catastrophe of 1,000 worlds? Would it make my people happy? I think not! My ways seem cruel to you, I'm sure. You do not understand that everything I do is to protect the simple, natural, ecological life my people lead. Before the age of terraforming, a monarch was responsible only for the human subjects of a given kingdom. Now a monarch can control the plants and animals as well, change the very water we drink, the very air we breathe, the total environment. That is what it means to be an Ecolog!" She had not raised her voice, but her tone carried a power and conviction that Briggs found almost impossible to oppose.

Yet still he said, "There are dangers. What you don't know *can* hurt you. For example—"

She laughed scornfully. "Dangers? Of course there are

dangers. But don't you suppose I have resources to deal with these dangers? Do you think I have lived for 300 years without learning anything, without making any preparations? My people live in a low-energy technology, but I do not. Never forget, offworlder, that you and I have fought a war."

"A war?"

"In the first moments of your visit to this planet I matched my technology against yours and won. I jammed your broadcast power transmission and you were unable to unjam it. You could not have known the principles of the technology I used, or you would either have not used broadcast power or you would have known, as I know, how to unjam it. Tell the truth, Commodore. You believed it was impossible to jam gravatic power transmissions, didn't you?"

He nodded sheepishly. "That's right."

"Then what is out there in your proud galactic empire that could possibly endanger me?"

'The Lorns," he blurted.

"Lorns?"

"The Lorns are a non-human, alien race. They and the humans are locked in a fight to the death as relentless as those insect battles your court watches on television. When the Lorns come upon a planet able to support life, they wipe that planet clean of every native life form down to the very germs and bacteria. Then they populate it with themselves and the slave-creatures they create by genetic manipulation. If the word evil has any meaning, they are evil!"

She sighed. "Not evil. Wise. They do what I should have done when I first came to this planet. I was too soft." She glanced at the sleeping ngaa. "I was too kind."

"But the Lorns will not be soft or kind to you or your people, and they may arrive here at any moment."

"Arrive here? Why here?" Her voice was again cold and grim.

"They may have followed us. . . ."

She became sarcastic. "I see we have one more thing to thank you for. Have you any more delightful surprises?"

"We can defend you against the Lorns!"

"I do not need your defense. If the Lorns come here I will defeat them as I defeated you."

"They won't land on your planet or try to establish communications. They'll simply attack."

"You did not establish communications from any benevolent motivation, Commodore Briggs. You wanted to use our computers. Tell me now, why did you want to use our computers?"

Briggs hesitated. Could he give her the truth? Something told him that, with her, nothing but the truth would do. She would see through any lie he might concoct. "Our ship's energy banks are almost empty. We have a device—the same device we use to broadcast power—by which we can tap energy out of a star. We were going to refuel from your sun, but there was a chance that if your sun was near a period of instability, our tap could trigger a nova."

"Trigger a nova?" The Ecolog sprang to her feet. "You were going to blow up our sun?"

Briggs tried to explain. "We wouldn't make the tap if there was any danger to human or other sentient life forms, and you were here. We had to analyze the data and determine exactly the probability of nova. If there was too much risk, we wouldn't do it. But our own computer had been damaged in an earlier skirmish with the Lorns, so we—"

Her fists were clenched. Her body shook with suppressed fury. "So you thought you could borrow ours!"

"Yes, that's right. It was the only way we could avoid endangering you and your—"

"Tell me, Commodore. In this earlier skirmish with the Lorns, did you defeat them?"

"No, but—"

"If you did not defeat them then, how can you be sure you'll defeat them in your next encounter?"

"We can't be sure, but—"

"You can't be sure? You tell me you've led some sort of interstellar monsters to our doorstep. You tell me you have to risk blowing up our sun in order to combat them. And then you tell me that you can't be sure of defeating them?"

Briggs smiled nervously. "I guess it doesn't sound too good, but with your cooperation we can reduce the real risk. . . ." He felt suddenly old and tired. His arguments rang hollow even in his own ears.

Her voice rose. "I will reduce the risk, all right! It is you who are the risk! It is you who constitute the greatest danger my people have ever faced! You, personally! I cannot allow you to communicate with your mothership. I cannot allow you to run around free. I cannot allow you to go on living!"

With two strides she reached the edge of her platform. Her slender fingers reached out and tugged on a bellcord. Briggs put his foot on the first step leading up to her. She whirled, sword in hand. Beside him the pet ngaa awoke with a start and stood up, fangs bared, fingers flexing, yellow eyes glaring at him.

Briggs, unarmed, halted instantly.

She brandished her saber expertly, like a master swordsman. "I give you a choice, Commodore. Die now or die later!" Her voice was challenging, exultant.

He sighed and said wearily, "I don't mind waiting."

Behind him he heard the heavy doors burst open and the running footsteps of the guards rushing forward to drag him away.

CAPTAIN Klain stood apart from the other conspirators. Omen, Sewall, Nord and Wing were speaking together in low voices, huddled near the sphere that housed the holographic model of the galaxy. Klain could not hear what they were saying. He did not want to hear! If there was something important, they would tell him, force him to listen. In the meantime he could not bear their trivial nit-picking, their worries, their paranoia.

His mind was riveted to the weapon in his belt, hidden under his cloak. The others could talk all they pleased; it was Klain who would act.

He knew the other conspirators were asking each other if Briggs had informed on them, or if the Ecolog had somehow guessed the plot on her own. Perhaps they were wondering if the Ecolog would kill them quickly or slowly. To Klain it no longer mattered. He would do what he must, yet it would be almost a relief to be caught, to not have to do it after all.

Suddenly he heard the sound of running booted feet. Surprised, he turned to see a squad of riflemen jogging through the front entrance in formation. *They're coming for us*, he thought without emotion.

From the round-eyed expressions on the other plotters' faces, he guessed they were thinking the same thing.

Klain stood, half-smiling, and watched the soldiers come toward him.

They came.

They passed.

Klain heard the others sigh with relief as the soldiers continued on down the hall to the room where the off-worlders were being held.

And now Marcia of Green and Angora appeared.

"Marcia!" Klain called. "What's going on?"

"We can't stop to talk," Marcia answered briskly. "The Ecolog has ordered the imprisonment of all the off-worlders."

"The imprisonment?" Klain was dumbfounded.

"And the execution," added Angora as she went by.

Klain stared after them. A fat hand clutched his arm.

"If the Ecolog kills the offworlders, it will spoil everything," said Omen in dismay.

Wing said, "It's not too late to call the whole thing off."

"No, no," said Omen hurriedly. "We may never have another chance. And have you considered how the off-worlders' friends will react to her butchery? They're up above us somewhere, you know, in a space vessel armed with weapons we've probably never even heard of. The Ecolog must be insane to risk their displeasure! Don't you see? She is, in effect, committing suicide and taking the whole planet with her."

Nord turned to Captain Klain and said in a low voice, "We can't delay the assassination any longer. She must be dead before—"

"Calm yourselves, gentlemen." Omen was sweating profusely. "The offworlders are still alive, are they not? And Lady Marcia said they would be imprisoned before being executed. The Ecolog must be planning a public execution, and for that she will need onlookers. You know the habits of the court. Almost everyone sleeps away the morning. That means the offworlders have at least until tomorrow noon!"

Wing nodded thoughtfully. "That makes sense."

"We must proceed calmly," said Omen, "but we must proceed. Captain Klain, when do you think you can get a private audience with the Ecolog?"

Klain answered numbly, "I don't know."

The riflemen were emerging once again from the room at the end of the hall. They had the offworlders with them. And someone else.

Klain said with surprise, "Look! Mara is being arrested too."

Klain left the knot of conspirators and started toward the troops. "Halt, there! Halt, I say!"

The soldiers halted.

Marcia of Green and Angora bustled up to him.

"You can't interfere here," said Marcia. "These troops are acting under direct orders from the Ecolog."

"But you're making a mistake." He gestured toward

Mara, who stood in the midst of the offworlders watching him with sullen eyes. "That girl there is one of us. She's no outlander!"

"She used to be one of us," Marcia corrected him primly. She turned to the soldiers. "What are you waiting for? Forward march!"

The soldiers obeyed.

"Halt!" cried Klain.

The soldiers ignored him, though some looked frightened. They knew as well as Klain that an order from a woman takes precedence over an order from a man, even if that man is the Ecolog's second-in-command.

Lady Marcia and Angora trotted along behind the troops. Klain followed.

"I'll take this matter up with the Ecolog," he said.

"Do you have an appointment with her?" demanded Marcia of Green.

"No, but—"

Angora said, "We may be able to arrange—"

Marcia broke in angrily, "We'll arrange nothing!"

Angora turned on her and screamed, "Who do you think you are?"

Marcia of Green did not reply, only smiled and continued on her way.

Angora, however, hung back with Klain. She took his hand and patted it. "I understand, Captain. Lady Marcia has no heart. She pushes everyone around, takes whatever she wants. . . ." Angora was on the verge of tears. "But never mind. I'll help you. I'll get you in to see the Ecolog."

She led him off in the opposite direction from the one taken by the troops.

THE Ecolog's voice was weary. "What is it, Angora?"

"Captain Klain wants to speak with you."

Klain saw the masked face turn in his direction, as he stood in the half-opened doorway. The blue eyes behind the slits were puzzled, questioning. "Tomorrow. . . ." said the Ecolog.

Angora's voice lowered, became confidential. "It's a matter of the heart."

The Ecolog chuckled. "Very well." She opened wide the door.

Klain felt the weapon in his belt, the strange offworlder pistol, pressing against his belly. The gun seemed to have grown, to have become so huge the Ecolog could not fail to see it, even under his cloak.

Angora said, "Good night, Your Majesty."

The Ecolog said, "Good night, Angora."

Angora departed. Klain stepped through the door. The Ecolog closed it.

The pet ngaa, sprawled on the floor, raised its head to eye him suspiciously. The air was thick with its smell.

"Could we go out on the balcony? The smell. . . ." To his own ears his voice sounded false, lying, but the Ecolog seemed to notice nothing unusual.

"All right, Klain," she answered.

She opened the intricately carved doors that led out onto the balcony. A light gust of wind caught the sleeves of her delicate blue gown as she stepped outside. She said softly, "The wind is picking up. Is your dirigible in the hangar?"

"No, but it's well tied down." He followed her through the doorway.

"I should have known you had everything under control. You always do." She walked to the heavy marble railing and looked down at the desert, her back to him. The sky was cloudless, the Galaxy brilliant.

He carefully closed the doors and latched them. They were sturdy. The ngaa would not be able to break through them by force. *But the creature has fingers*, he thought. *It can turn the doorknob.*

She said softly, "There are so many fools at court.

Women like that silly Angora, men like that pompous blimp Omen. I need someone like you, someone I can depend on. We've gone through a lot together, haven't we?"

"Yes, My Lady."

She shook her head slowly, sighing. He watched the back of her neck. Bare skin showed there. The pistol could probably pierce clothing easily enough, but on bare skin it would be certain to hit the mark.

"There have been rebellions," she went on. "We fought side by side. There have been earthquakes, fires, droughts. We worked together. We worked hard. We made life go on whether it wanted to or not."

"Yes, My Lady."

"Remember the wild ngaa hunts?"

"I remember."

"Remember the nights when we moored the dirigible to the rocks in the wilderness somewhere and camped out?"

"Yes."

She laughed softly. "We've done almost everything, at one time or another. Most of the time I've been happy, or at least too busy to ask whether I was happy or not. I don't know if I ever asked you this before, but have you been happy?"

He paused, then said, his voice shaking slightly. "Yes, I've been happy."

"You didn't miss . . . the physical side of love?"

"I've had the ladies of the court to supply that."

"I know." She shrugged. "I might as well admit I've been jealous sometimes. Yes, it is the truth. But I know I can't expect a man like you to take a vow of celibacy. You have your needs. I recognize that. So if you wish to discuss what that silly woman Angora calls 'a matter of the heart,' you can be frank with me. I'll do what I can for you."

"Her name is Mara." His hand closed on the butt of the gun.

"The one who drinks?"

"Yes." His finger found the trigger.

"I would have hoped you could do better, Klain."

"She's . . . not so bad." He drew the pistol slowly out of his belt. His cloak still concealed it. "But sometimes she does foolish things, because of the drink. She's gotten herself arrested now, along with the offworlders."

The Ecolog laughed her low melodious laugh. "Is that all?"

"She could be executed with them." The gun was outside his cape. He raised it, took aim.

"So I will release her, my dear. You know I can deny you nothing! I want your mind free now, without worry or bitterness over some little playmate. There may be troubled times ahead. The offworlders have friends—yes—and enemies we must contend with. Life may not be so peaceful." Her head had begun to turn toward him. In a moment she would see him.

His hand shook violently. But what did that matter? This gun shot missiles that would seek out their target, missiles that could not miss. He need only pull the trigger.

But he could not.

She caught sight of the pistol and became motionless. When she was still she was somehow more still than anyone else.

His mind was awash with images. He and the Ecolog, pilot and copilot of the dirigible. He and the Ecolog at parties, whispering their opinions of the guests to each other. He and the Ecolog supervising the construction of buildings, planning things, directing things. He and the Ecolog talking quietly in the evening, after everyone else had gone.

The Ecolog spoke calmly, quietly. "Do you want to vote against me? Go ahead. My suffering will not last long." She drew back her blue gown to expose her slender throat, her shoulders.

Klain began to weep. At first there were only sniffles and the wet sensation of tears running down his cheeks, but as he gradually lowered his weapon he was wracked with a series of horrible tearing sobs that built up, little by little, to a final strangled cry of despair.

He stumbled forward, half-blind, and thrust the weapon into her hands.

"Take it," he cried. "Use it on me. You have every right to!"

She took it, examined it thoughtfully, caressed the handle. Her forefinger closed around the trigger.

Then, to his astonishment, she laughed. It was the same low melodious laugh as always, if anything a little more warm and playful than usual. With one hand she slipped the gun inside her flowing blue gown; with the other she reached out and touched his cheek.

"I think not, my darling captain," she said. "At this moment you are the one person in this court whose loyalty is proven."

THE holding cell was large but uncomfortable; cut into the bedrock beneath the palace its walls, floor and ceiling were hard, cold and impenetrable. There was no furniture. The door was made from a single slab of steel broken only by a tiny, square window at eye level through which dimly streamed a yellow, flickering lamplight from the hall. This was the room's sole illumination. The air was motionless and bore the subtle odor of ancient dust and sweat and urine. The silence was disturbed only by the sound of breathing and the distant murmur and occasional laughter of the guards.

Seated on the floor, backs to the wall, were Commodore Briggs, Lieutenant Mike Phillips, Garbage, the seven crewmen from the *Corregidor*, and the sullen Mara. There were others in the cell with them; Briggs could see dark, slow-moving figures on the opposite side of the room.

Briggs sighed and turned to Garbage. He said softly, "I feel I'd like to talk to you, but I really can't think of anything to say."

She answered, "Don't say anything you wouldn't want a spy to hear." She nodded toward Mara.

Mara said without emotion, "I'm no spy."

"I don't know any other reason for you being here," Garbage said.

"That's right," said Mara tonelessly. "You don't know."

Briggs said, "Tell me, Mara, why did you join us?"

"To die," said Mara, still without emotion.

"To die?" Briggs was puzzled.

Mara explained, "I knew the Ecolog would have to kill you. You don't fit in. None of you do."

"Do you?" asked Garbage. "Do you fit in?"

Mara shrugged. "Maybe. Maybe not. I'm the same as everybody except . . . well, I've wanted to die for a long time, to kill myself. I mean, think about it. No more hangovers! But suicide was always too much work. You know, I didn't care about it all that much, one way or the other." She brightened. "But if I'm executed along with you, I'll be a scandal, a wonderful scandal. The court will never stop talking about me! They'll never stop wondering why I did it. I'll be immortal in my way. It's not as good as the Ecolog's way, but, well. . . ." She shrugged again. "Finally I'll be somebody!"

Garbage said mockingly, "You won't be at all."

Mara drew away from her angrily. "Are you trying to spoil my fun?"

Garbage's voice was weary. "No. Never mind. You're no crazier than the rest of us. I didn't really have to come to Abbutututikan. Neither did you, Commodore."

Briggs spoke sadly. "That's where you're wrong. I did have to come. A soldier does what he must, not what he likes. But I deeply regret dragging you in here with me."

"Dragging me?" Garbage sat up haughtily. "No man drags me anywhere I do not want to go. You fool! Back in the desert, when nobody could see but me, I could have abandoned you anytime and left you for the ngaas to dine on. That was what I'd planned to do the moment you caught me."

Briggs asked gently, "Why didn't you do it?"

She looked at him in the dim, flickering light with an odd, enigmatic expression on her face. "I saw something in you, Commodore, something I needed, something this planet needs." She chose her words with care. "You did not appear to be a man who takes a vote before he decides what to do. You did not appear to be a man who looks around before he decides what to think. Once, perhaps, there were many men like you, but now they are nearly extinct. Instead we are surrounded by boys. Some are young boys with long, girlish hair. Some are old boys with bald, empty heads. All are very, very fashionable." Her voice had become bitter and sarcastic, but now it became low, warm and melodious again. "You are someone who does not often say yes, but when he does, means it. You are someone who needs little, but never gives that little away. You are someone who loves peace, but will kill to defend what is yours. You are neither cruel nor kind. You do what needs doing, and move on. Yes, Commodore, I saw something in you, and I see it still."

Briggs felt flattered, embarrassed. "Well, thank you. I . . . I'm at a loss for words. If you saw something in me—"

"What I saw," she said softly, "was a tool."

"A tool?" Briggs shifted uneasily.

She chuckled. "A tool for conquest. Shall I amuse you? Are you able to laugh at what is called gallows humor? Of course you are! I saw in you the means to conquer the Ecolog and revive this dying civilization. What? You're not laughing? You disappoint me, Commodore. It's all for the best that we did not win. Our court would be such a bore!"

Briggs took her hands in his. He sighed heavily. "It does appear I've been somewhat of a disappointment."

"Too bad," she whispered. She closed her eyes and

leaned over, presenting her lips to be kissed. Briggs, flustered, hunched down awkwardly and kissed her.

Mike Phillips said ironically, "Do you take this man to be your lawfully wedded husband?" He paused. His next words were even more bittersweet. "Until death do you part?"

The kiss was over. Garbage said, "What's a husband?"

An angry bass voice boomed out of the darkness. "Will you shut up over there? I'm trying to sleep!"

Another voice answered, "Shut up yourself! Tomorrow you can sleep forever!"

There were sounds of a scuffle, the thud of blows, grunts, cries and shouted blasphemies.

Outside in the hallway Briggs heard running footsteps. The face of a guard appeared at the little window in the door. It was a crude but good-natured face. "Quiet in there! Quiet I say!"

The booming voice called out, "What're ya gonna do, eh? Kill me?"

This remark was greeted with a chorus of harsh laughter, but nevertheless the fight ceased and the cell quieted down.

Briggs said to the guard, "Hey, there. Can you answer a question?"

"What question?" said the guard with suspicion.

"Will I be allowed a lawyer?"

"A lawyer?" The guard looked blank.

"At my trial."

"Trial? There won't be no trial. The Ecolog kills men like a gardener pulls weeds." He favored Briggs with a yellow-toothed grin and was about to turn away from the window. Suddenly his eyes widened. "Who. . . ." he began. A large, heavy-bladed knife hissed through the air and buried itself in his throat. His face retained a look of surprise as he fell out of sight with a heavy thud.

Briggs sprang to his feet.

A different face appeared at the window, round and fat and exultant.

"Omen!" said Briggs.

"I trust you're feeling properly revolutionary," said the fat man teasingly.

Briggs hesitated briefly before replying, "Yes, I guess so."

The key rattled in the lock. The door swung open with a creak.

Briggs bounded through the opening into the corridor, almost tripping over the guard. Sewall was waiting there, eyes glittering with exhilaration, and in his hand Briggs saw . . . the claymore!

"A humble gift," said the little man, bowing slightly.

Briggs snatched the ancient Scottish weapon and swished it in an arc around his head.

Nord and Wing stood nearby, also armed with swords, and behind them was a murmuring crowd of similarly armed men. Omen was handing swords and knives to the former inmates of the holding cell as they emerged shambling and blinking into the light.

Briggs frowned. "Omen! Where are the rifles, pistols and stinger guns?"

Omen was apologetic. "There were only knives and swords in the Royal Armory."

"But aren't there modern weapons around here somewhere?"

"Of course."

"Well, where are they then?"

"The Ecolog's troops have them all."

CHAPTER 8

Too much sun and not enough sleep. That was a bad combination. Commodore Briggs felt tired and ill. His bones ached. His head ached. At times he was dizzy and nauseous. Sitting down in the cell he had felt better, almost normal, but now that he was in motion his body seemed to cry out at every step, "Slow down. Stop. Lie down."

He was climbing a dark, winding stone stairway that seemed to have no end. There had been no election, but somehow Briggs had found himself thrust into the role of leader. Close behind him panted the corpulent Omen, followed by Mike Phillips, Sewall, Wing, Nord, Mara and the others. The entire force could not have numbered more than 50. Around each right arm was tied a bit of yellow cloth, the makeshift insignia of the tiny ragtag army.

The claymore, dangling in its scabbard from his belt, seemed twice as heavy as he remembered, and his knee-length boots seemed made of lead, yet somehow he managed to keep going.

Omen whispered, "Surprise! That's what will win for us. Klain will assassinate the Ecolog while we take out her personal guard."

Briggs thought about the euphemism "take out." What a world of murder and bloodshed it covered up! Briggs's mind recoiled from the prospect, but the greater horror of the Lorns goaded him on. This way some would die, yes, but the entire planet would not be wiped clean of life.

But did they have a chance against the Ecolog's modern weapons? Briggs thought so. He knew how, all through history, the element of surprise and the use of guerrilla tactics had often nullified the advantage of superior arms. Still, it would be nice to have some guns.

Briggs said, "Omen, are you sure no firearms are available?"

145

Omen wheezed, "I told you where we'd find them. The Ecolog's troops have them. If we want guns we'll have to fight for 'em. At the head of these stairs is the barracks."

Briggs whispered, "Why didn't you tell me?" This was the first Briggs had heard about any barracks.

Omen frowned, finger to lips. "Ssh. It's around the next bend." Above them appeared a broad passageway.

They came in sight of a plain wooden door. It was closed, and from the other side could be heard the low murmur of conversation. Briggs drew his claymore, waited while the others followed suit, then tried the latch. It was unlocked. The door opened slightly and a shaft of light appeared.

With a cry Briggs kicked the door open and leaped into the room.

All around him were the Ecolog's troops in various stages of undress, some asleep on the long lines of bunks, some standing around with cups of a steaming beverage in their hands. Heads turned. Eyes widened. A slim man standing directly in Briggs's path reached for a sword that hung sheathed from a nearby bedpost.

Briggs chopped him down with a single stroke of the claymore.

Another man shouted a warning to his comrades. Briggs lunged forward and ran him through.

A third man turned to flee. Briggs stabbed him between the shoulder blades.

A fourth man tried to attack Briggs with his bare hands and died screaming.

As Briggs's forces poured through the doorway, hacking, stabbing and slashing, the Ecolog's guards seemed at first paralyzed with shock, on the verge of panic, as if—as was quite possible—this was their first experience of battle. Briggs fought his way down the center aisle between two rows of bunks; Omen followed him, cutting the throats of those who slept or were only half-awake. Nord and Wing and Sewall sprinted down the other aisles, red swords flying. The guards were falling like wheat before a scythe.

Briggs looked around for guns. None were in sight.

Was Omen mistaken, or had the fat rascal lied?

The guards were beginning to recover from the initial shock of attack and put up a token resistance. Perhaps it was better that they had no guns. They were trouble enough with nothing but swords. A counterattack had begun, and Briggs's forces were brought to a standstill, forced back. The air was filled with the clash of blade on blade, shouts, screams, running footsteps, groans, the crash of overturned cots, and a chorus of oaths, blasphemies and hoarse obscenities.

Hand to hand fighting is hard, hot, hideous work. It was made no easier for Briggs by his sick sense of failure; he'd failed to find another way, a peaceful way. He was not like Omen, who seemed to love this battle, who had begun to sing tunelessly as his knife stabbed and cut, or like Sewall who laughed with delight as he swung his scimitar.

Someone's blood spattered in Briggs's eyes, blinding him for an instant, making him want to vomit. He wiped his eyes with his forearm and fought on. His mind cried out to him to stop, but his arm, trained in a thousand mock encounters, carried out its task, doing all the right things, making all the right moves; habit was like an androit demon possessing him. He was weary and afraid and sick, but his arm was a tireless robot programed to kill. It sliced, slashed and maimed all on its own, never once asking permission.

Briggs watched himself as if from a great distance, as if in a dream.

A frightened voice cried out, "We surrender!"

As Briggs looked toward the voice, he saw a man with the white stripes of superior rank on his sleeve. "We surrender!" shouted the man again.

The skirmish was over.

Slowly Briggs lowered his claymore.

LIEUTENANT Phillips clutched his arm, blood oozing through his fingers, while Commodore Briggs applied a tourniquet made from Mike's yellow insignia-cloth. Mike was in pain, but managed a wan smile.

Wing and Nord, unhurt except for a few minor cuts, had been helping the wounded and counting the dead; now they approached the cot where Mike sat. Briggs glanced in their direction, noticed how pale they were.

"What's wrong?" Briggs demanded.

"Your men, sir," answered Wing. "They're dead. All seven."

Briggs swayed, eyes closed. This was something he hadn't expected. Seven men from the *Corregidor* . . . his friends. They'd come a long way to die for something they probably didn't even understand.

Phillips said softly, "They didn't have any training for this kind of fighting." Phillips, who had often served as a fencing partner for Briggs, had come through alive. Briggs thought bitterly, *It's my fault they're dead. If I'd trained them. . . .*

With an effort he pulled himself together. "How do we stand otherwise, Wing?"

"Over half our force is out, either dead or too badly wounded to do us any good. I'd say we have around 20 or 21 able to fight."

Briggs shook his head worriedly. "Not good. We were outnumbered and outgunned before, but now. . . ." He glanced at Omen on the other side of the room. Omen and Sewall were tying up the prisoners.

"Omen," called Briggs. "Where are those guns you were talking about?"

Omen answered with inane cheerfulness. "They're not here."

Briggs swore under his breath, then called, "I can see they're not here. Where are they?"

Omen smiled sheepishly. "I don't really know, Commodore."

Briggs almost lost his temper. "You never did know, did you?"

Omen laughed. "You guessed it."

"You fat, stupid, half-witted——" Briggs began.

Omen broke in. "What are you angry about? Don't you understand that we've won? We've taken out the guard, and Captain Klain has killed the Ecolog. We've won! It's all over but the mopping up."

"Do you know for a fact that Klain has killed the Ecolog?"

Omen shrugged. "Not exactly for a fact." He brightened. "But that was his assignment."

A loudspeaker over the door suddenly beeped loudly. Startled, Briggs turned to stare at it. A tense voice began speaking.

"This is Captain Klain."

Omen said gleefully. "You see? Klain's in control now. The Ecolog is dead. Long live King Klain!"

Klain's voice continued, "Arm yourselves. I repeat, arm yourselves. A conspiracy against our beloved Ecolog has been uncovered, led by High Councillor Omen in collaboration with the offworlders. The offworlders have escaped from prison with his help, along with a number of condemned criminals, and are roaming at large. If you see any——"

"Traitor!" screamed Omen hysterically as he hurled a knife across the room to bury itself in the speaker with a thump. The offending voice ceased in mid-phrase.

Omen was howling, "He went over! I was a fool to trust him! I should have known!" He pounded himself on the head with his fat fists.

"We're not dead yet," snapped Briggs.

"We might as well be," wailed Omen.

"The guns!" shouted Briggs. "We still have a chance if we can find the guns!"

"I don't know where they are!" Omen was on the verge of cracking. "I told you that!"

Sewall had been eyeing the prisoners and now drew his scimitar. "Perhaps," he said softly, "one of these gentlemen will be kind enough to tell us."

Wing grinned. "Now we'll find out. . . ."

He never finished his sentence. A bullet buried itself in his face. As the sound of the shot echoed through the room, Commodore Briggs spun to face the open doorway. A lone rifleman crouched there, half-hidden by the doorjamb, with the largest rifle Briggs had ever seen.

Boom! The big gun went off again.

Nord screamed and fell clutching his stomach.

The rifle swung, aimed at Briggs. *Please, no,* he thought numbly. With a whoop Sewall the Scout raised his scimitar and charged. "Yaaaaaah!"

The rifle wavered, swung away from Briggs to aim at Sewall.

Another explosion and the little man fell in a lifeless heap.

The echo of the shot covered the sound of running bare feet. A small figure in a thin white rayon shift darted toward the doorway, long, black, tangled hair streaming behind.

Mara!

The gun swung toward her, but not in time. In a final desperate leap she was through the doorway and on top of the rifleman, her dagger thrust into his chest.

He gasped once, then lay still.

She looked up, saw that all eyes were upon her, drew herself up proudly and shouted, "Can't you men ever do anything right?"

With that she stooped, snatched up the heavy rifle and scampered off into the darkness beyond the doorway.

ARM in arm, Captain Klain and the Ecolog descended the broad marble staircase outside her throne room. Her pet ngaa appeared in the doorway and trotted after them on its rear four feet, its frontmost feet—or were they hands—

raised and flexing. The scratching of its claws on the stone steps echoed through the immense, circular hall; the smell of decaying flowers filled the air.

The Ecolog was, as always, beautiful and horrible, graceful and demonic. Her diaphanous blue gown drifted behind her like mist; the rubies, sapphires, diamonds and emeralds in the pommel of her scimitar and in her platinum mask caught gleams and flashes from the torches, and her bare arms seemed to glow with a pale light of their own.

At her side, Captain Klain looked haggard and worried, more gaunt and haunted than ever, his heavy blue cloak swirling around him, his knee-high black boots catching the lamplight in their muted sheen.

A woman soldier, the night guard, saluted as they passed, then stepped back a pace to allow the ngaa plenty of room.

At the foot of the stairs the couple halted.

Klain said gently, "You must hide. If you go to the dorms of the special girls, no one will ever be able to find you."

She stood away from him, head cocked to one side, holding his hands. "That's not how chess is played, my darling captain. It's the queen who goes forth to battle. She's the strongest and most dangerous piece on the board. It is the king who hangs back behind the pawns and hides." She laughed.

"This is no game!"

"Everything is a game."

She started toward the exit. Reluctantly, he followed. Suddenly the doors ahead of them burst open. The Ecolog drew her sword in a flash.

Angora, in the doorway, emitted a little scream. Her hand flew to the base of her throat in an unconscious gesture of defensiveness. "Oh, Your Majesty! You frightened me!"

The Ecolog said tensely, "Klain, is she one of them?"

Klain shook his head. "No, not her."

The scimitar lowered. The Ecolog demanded with suspicion, "What are you doing here?"

Angora stepped through the doorway. "I saw your lights were on when I was out in the garden. I thought I could talk to you about something."

"What kind of a something?" said the Ecolog.

"A matter of the heart."

Angrily the Ecolog sheathed her sword. "Not now."

"It's a decision only you can make." Angora's voice had taken on a note of pleading.

"Not now," repeated the Ecolog, more loudly.

Angora explained anyway. "Lady Marcia of the House of Green and I have been sharing a certain man, a techman named Morgan. It's not working out. She takes more than her share of his time and—"

Lady Marcia appeared in the doorway. "Don't listen to her, Your Majesty. That's not true!"

Klain snapped, "What do you expect the Ecolog to do about it?"

Angora said desperately. "The Ecolog can choose for us. She can give Morgan to one of us once and for all. Morgan is right outside this door, waiting for your decision."

Klain thought, *What is this? A joke? A trick?* "Angora! Lady Marcia! Don't you know there's a revolution under way? Don't you know our lives are in danger?"

Angora looked shocked. "I heard you talking on the loudspeaker, of course."

Lady Marcia added, "But what does that have to do with us?"

Angora finished, "We're not political."

The woman soldier was approaching. "Are these women bothering you, Your Majesty?"

Before the Ecolog could answer, there was a loud boom and a scream from beyond the door, followed by the sound of running boots. A young man in a red tunic burst through the door, tall, muscular and so handsome he was almost pretty, even with his face contorted with terror.

"Here's Morgan now," said Angora proudly.

Morgan ran past her without stopping, shouting, "There's a madwoman out there with a rifle! She shot at me!" From the foot of the stairs he shrieked, "Help!" Then he began bounding up the steps.

Marcia of Green and Angora turned around instantly and, one behind the other, blocked the door with their bodies. "Don't worry, Morgan," Angora began firmly. "We won't let—"

Boom!

Angora and Lady Marcia fell together. One bullet had passed through both their bodies.

Morgan had almost reached the top of the stairs.

Boom!

His torn body formed one final beautiful arch; then it tumbled awkwardly down the steps.

Boom!

The woman soldier spun around and fell in a heap.

Mara appeared in the doorway, her dark eyes glittering with an unholy glee, a huge smoking rifle clutched in her slender fingers. She saw the Ecolog, aimed at her.

The Ecolog shot first.

Snick! A hairline of fire, slightly curved, arced from the stinger pistol to Mara's throat. A tiny dart, hardly more than a needle, buried itself in Mara's flesh.

Mara's face clouded, relaxed into its habitual expression, a sullen, resentful pout. The rifle fell from her hands with a clatter on the stone floor. She collapsed into a kneeling position before pitching forward onto her face.

The Ecolog ran lightly to her and crouched to feel for a pulse.

Captain Klain glanced uneasily toward the doorway where Lady Marcia and Angora lay. "Let's get out of here," he said. "There may be others right behind."

"Just a minute. Ah, yes. She's dead."

The Ecolog stood up.

Klain said, "Why did you take her pulse?"

The Ecolog caressed the stinger pistol. "I wanted to be sure this weapon carried real poison. The darts could have nothing in them but tranquilizer or knockout shots."

"Shall we take the rifle?"

She shook her head. "It's too noisy for hide-and-seek." She turned toward her pet ngaa and spoke to it in its own language of squeaks, whistles and pops. Klain was surprised. He hadn't known she could do that.

The creature sat on its haunches and slowly nodded its ponderous head.

"What did you tell him?" asked Klain.

"I told him to stay here and stop anyone who tries to follow me." She started up the steps.

Klain went with her. "Will he do it?"

"Of course he will. He loves me, doesn't he?"

Klain knew where they were going. There was a secret exit on the other side of the throne room. As he hurried up the stairs he glanced back once at Mara. He thought, *Poor little idiot.*

He could not know this was what she'd always wanted.

WITH some vague idea of taking the rifle from Mara, Omen had set off in pursuit, but she was far more light-footed and soon outdistanced him. When he'd left the guardroom, he'd had the distinct impression that some of the others were with him, or at least not far behind. Now, abruptly, he realized he was alone. Mara had vanished down the shadowy corridor ahead of him and—he stopped and turned around to make sure—no one followed him.

He stood, puffing and wheezing and sweating, as the full enormity of his position dawned on him; then he thrust his hand into his sleeve, groping for one of the many knives he always carried. He had thrown his last one. He was totally unarmed.

He took a few steps back the way he had come.

But wait! Was that the sound of distant marching feet?

Omen's so-called army did not march; it slunk. These marchers must be the Ecolog's troops.

He turned on his heel and began slogging down the hallway in the direction Mara had disappeared and away from the steadily increasing sound of marching feet.

Things were definitely not going the way he had planned it at all. A tear trickled down his fat cheek, and with effort, he suppressed a sob. There was nothing left to do, it seemed, but keep out of sight as long as possible, though sooner or later the Ecolog would find him. Didn't she own the whole planet? And when she caught him, what would she do? He had visions of himself being turned on a spit over a roaring fire, roasted alive, at a gala barbecue. What a grand party it would be! Everyone who was anyone would be there. Or at least everyone who had remained loyal.

Omen tried to run faster, but could do no more than continue to wobble along, his breath coming in hoarse, terrified gasps.

It was all Klain's fault!

The thought of Captain Klain brought Omen up short.

Of course! That must be where Mara was going with the rifle . . . to do the job Klain had failed to do—kill the Ecolog.

Klain set off again, but now he had a destination. Mara must have been headed for the throne room and the Ecolog's quarters. Very well. Omen would go there too. Perhaps he could help Mara, or at least share her victory. A wild, desperate hope leaped to life within him. If the Ecolog was dead, everything would be all right!

Omen knew the back passages, the out-of-the-way halls and staircases. He knew how to reach the throne room without being seen. A lunatic smile illuminated his round features.

He heard a shot!

The sound came from the direction of the throne room, not far away. Was the Ecolog dead?

Omen slowed to a jog, listening.

A second shot echoed through the gloomy halls, then a third and a fourth. The echo died away. Omen grinned. Four shots! Even the Ecolog could not survive four shots. Or perhaps one or two had been used to put that turncoat Klain out of the way. So much the better!

Ahead a door stood ajar. Flickering torchlight streamed through.

Omen slowed.

Two corpses were lying in a heap together in the doorway. Omen recognized Lady Marcia of the House of Green and Angora. The smell of gunsmoke hung in the air, and another smell. Roses!

Puzzled, Omen leaned over the bodies and peered in. He saw the marble staircase leading up to the throne room. The throne-room door was open.

Halfway down the stairs lay a dead man, quietly bleeding.

At the foot of the stairs was a dead woman soldier.

And there, not more than a few steps away, was Mara. Mara was not bloody like the others. Perhaps she was only unconscious. He looked closer. No, she was not breathing.

Near her hand lay the big rifle.

Omen stared at it for a long time.

He listened. There was no sound but his own labored breathing and the hiss and sputter of the torches.

As he studied the grim tableau, nothing moved in the flickering shadows. Was someone there he could not see?

He sniffed the curious smell of flowers and frowned.

His gaze moved once again to the gun. If he could get that gun. . . .

Carefully he stepped over Marcia and Angora, walked slowly toward Mara and leaned over. His gross fingers closed over the cold steel rifle. He picked it up and, with a grunt, resumed a standing position. He examined the

magazine, which extended into the weapon's stock. Three
bullets left. One for Klain, one for the Ecolog, and one for
luck. He smiled, his soul at peace.

Then he saw the ngaa.

The creature had been crouched in a shadow, as still as
stone. Even now Omen could see no trace of movement,
only the vague black outline of the animal.

Omen stepped backward, very slowly.

The thing's head moved slightly and the torchlight
reflected in its yellow eyes, making them glow like the
jewels in the Ecolog's mask.

Slowly Omen raised the rifle and took aim.

Slowly he squeezed the trigger.

The gun jerked in his hands, almost escaping him. Its
explosion was deafening and set the room thundering with
echoes.

With a startled cry the ngaa tumbled over on its back,
four legs and two arms thrashing. Omen gave a wordless
shout of triumph.

But the ngaa was not dead. Almost instantly it rolled
back onto its feet, fangs bared, hissing and clicking. Claws
scratching the stone floor, it advanced into the light. Omen
saw a dent and a white scratch on the animal's bony armor
where the bullet had bounced off. The impact had knocked
the ngaa off its feet, but it was otherwise unhurt.

Omen aimed again and fired.

This time the ngaa did not lose its footing, just staggered
slightly and kept on coming, its huge jaws opening wide.

Omen dropped the gun and closed his eyes, thinking defiantly, *I don't need to see this.*

But he couldn't shut out the smell.

Omen's last sensation was the overpowering, suffocating,
smothering stench of decaying roses.

COMMODORE Briggs had intended to run after Omen, but
as he left the guardroom, he heard footsteps on the stairs
leading up from the subterranean dungeons. He bounded

back into the room and signaled a warning, then stood in a half-crouch by the door, sword drawn.

A voice called out of the darkness, "We surrender!" A surprising note of suppressed mirth was in the tone.

Briggs frowned. Surrender? Why would anyone surrender to a tiny "army" of amateur revolutionaries armed with nothing but knives and swords? It must be a trick!

Briggs shrugged. They were done for anyway.

He bellowed, "Come forward and hand over your arms. Hands up and don't make any sudden moves."

At the head of the stairs a man appeared, one of the Ecolog's swordsmen, with a white stripe of command on the sleeve of his short-sleeved blue tunic. The man was grinning.

"What's so funny?" Briggs demanded.

"We were about to launch our own revolution when we heard about yours," the soldier answered.

More soldiers appeared behind the first, and more, and more. The first soldier stopped in front of Briggs. Mike Phillips, at Briggs's elbow, said, "How do we know you're telling the truth?"

The officer replied, "Because we don't have to lie. We could kill you all if we wanted to. We outnumber you by at least three to one." He had now advanced to a position where he could see Briggs's entire force—such as it was— through the doorway. "Why should we surrender if we're not telling the truth?"

Briggs slowly lowered his claymore. He had, however, one final question. "Why surrender at all?"

The officer said, "We had heard the Ecolog imprisoned you. We didn't like that. The civilians at court didn't care one way or the other, but we saw your arrival here as an opportunity for our civilization to end the three centuries of isolation that have turned our whole world into a kind of prison. We had planned to overthrow the Ecolog this very night, never dreaming you had the same idea. Now, when the other troops see that we, the Ecolog's personal swordsmen, have gone over to your side, I doubt if there's a single fighting man in Abbututtikan who won't surrender. It's a pity, though, you had to tangle with the guards." He gestured toward the scene of carnage in the guardroom. "I'm sure they would have come over too if I had beaten you to them."

Briggs said, "It was a mistake." He was thinking of his crewmen who need not have died.

"A mistake. Yes," the officer answered bleakly. He stepped forward and extended his hand. "But let's have no grudges, eh? No grudges on either side."

The two shook hands.

"No grudges," Briggs agreed. "I'm Commodore Abraham Briggs, in command of the starship *Corregidor*."

"And I'm Lieutenant Myron Marks. Where's that old fop, Omen?" A note of respect crept into Myron's voice. "I never dreamed he had the guts to try a coup."

Briggs gestured down the hall. "He ran off that way."

"Probably headed toward the Ecolog's chambers. Let's follow him." He called his men to form ranks.

Briggs said, "There's no need to kill the Ecolog now, is there?" He sheathed the claymore.

Myron answered, "No, I was thinking we might form an honor guard to escort her to the dungeons."

The Commodore was thinking fast. "But Omen doesn't know the situation. He'll still think he has to kill her. Damn! That will make one more needless death." He turned to Garbage and demanded, "Do you know the way to the Ecolog's chambers?"

She nodded. "Of course I do."

"Lead me there," said Briggs.

Garbage was reluctant. "Maybe it would be better if she wasn't around to—"

"You promised to lead me to her. Remember?" Briggs insisted.

She laughed. "I remember. Very well, let's go!"

She set off running, bare feet slapping on the stone.

Briggs followed. He was weary and sore, a lumbering shambling bear, but he knew he had to at least try to save the Ecolog's life.

"You're a fool, Briggs," the girl called back to him.

"I know," puffed Briggs. He kept on running.

Behind him Briggs heard Lieutenant Myron shout to his men, "Forward march!" The sound of marching feet echoed through the halls.

Briggs and Garbage ran in silence for a few minutes. The marching men were out of sight behind them, although they could still be plainly heard.

Suddenly, far ahead, Briggs heard a shot.

Thinking it was too late, he regretfully slowed his pace.

Then he heard a second shot, and a third, and a fourth.

A battle! The Ecolog must be still alive, fighting for her life! He again broke into a run.

Garbage led him up a circular stone staircase, around and around until he was dizzy, but he didn't stop.

Half a minute later he heard a fifth shot, and a sixth, much closer.

He rounded a corner and came in sight of a doorway. Garbage had halted there and was kneeling beside two bodies that lay partially blocking passage. The room beyond was lit by the dim light of imitation torches.

Garbage raised a warning hand, saying in a low voice, "It's Marcia and Angora. They've been gunned down. And do you smell what I smell?"

Briggs sniffed the air. "Gunsmoke and . . . roses. The ngaa?"

"That's right. The Ecolog's pet is somewhere around here."

Cautiously Briggs peeped through the door. "Mara's dead, too, on the floor," he whispered. "That gun she took is right beside her. Maybe that will hold off the ngaa."

Garbage grabbed his arm. "No it won't. Even a big gun like that won't penetrate the armor of an adult ngaa."

"What will?" he asked.

"A cannon."

"Then what can we do now?"

"Return the way we came and pray the ngaa doesn't track us."

Briggs was about to follow her advice when he heard a faint moan in the room. "Listen," he said softly. "That may be Omen, lying wounded and helpless."

She looked at him with exasperation and snapped, "And it may also be the ngaa burping."

Briggs pushed her gently aside and stepped over Marcia and Angora into the room.

"Come back!" Garbage whispered frantically.

He bent to pick up the gun.

He heard the moan again and glanced quickly in the direction of the sound. The ngaa was lying on its side, almost invisible in the shadows, possessively clutching the hideously mangled remains of Omen, the fat man. It was chewing thoughtfully and eyeing Briggs with an expression of cunning, as if to say, "I fooled you."

Moan, said the ngaa. Moan.

It was amazing how perfectly the creature could imitate a human voice.

The ngaa opened its mouth and spoke. "There are already too many humans on this planet, Commodore. You would bring more of them." Its voice was reedy and whistling but clearly understandable, its accent and style of speech a copy of the Ecolog's. "If the Ecolog remains in power, the human colony here will continue to decay. Eventually her kingdom will be too weak to fight us. We will be able to claim what is ours. And we will have 300 years of learning from you humans, studying your science while you mistake us for dumb beasts. We will perhaps sail from star to star as you do. We will perhaps be able to take revenge for all that you humans have done to us. You understand my position, I'm sure." Briggs could have sworn the creature was smiling. He could certainly see its long sharp teeth, yet its features were so inhuman he could not be sure. "I must, at all costs, head off anything that might revitalize your colony here, that might break our planet's isolation."

The ngaa scrambled to its feet, small disturbingly human hands opening and closing like twin spiders spinning webs. The smell of roses grew abruptly stronger, acting as a narcotic, making Briggs dizzy and stupid. How easy it would be to give up, drift aimlessly with that sweet-smelling tide, become passive and philosophical and sad. How relaxing to realize that, in the long view, nothing mattered all that much. His eyes fluttered closed, then opened again.

The ngaa was a dim black blur. Briggs could not seem to focus his eyes on it, but he knew it was coming closer. He could hear claws scraping on paving stones.

So easy not to care.

So easy.

Garbage screamed. Briggs's awareness returned with a jolt. Crouched and ready to spring, the ngaa snapped into sharp focus. The massive jaws opened wide, dagger-sharp teeth gleaming in the flickering light.

The ngaa leaped.

Briggs drew his claymore and thrust the blade deep into that gaping mouth, felt it pass though the palate, through cartilage and meat, into something softer, more yielding. The brain!

The full weight of the creature hit him like a boulder, sending him crashing to the floor. The ngaa was smaller than a man, hardly bigger than a wolf, but it was heavy, crushingly heavy.

The commodore was stunned, only half-conscious, but he managed to roll with the impact, managed to shift slightly so the ngaa did not fall on top of him. One of the deadly little hands clutched at his sleeve as he struggled away, but it succeeded only in ripping off a bit of cloth.

Briggs lay beside the ngaa as it twitched convulsively. The creature was dead. A thin trickle of blood began to flow from the massive mouth. Briggs was mildly surprised to see the blood was red, exactly like a man's. And he was relieved to note that the claymore, which now protruded from the roof of the ngaa's mouth, appeared undamaged.

Garbage ran to him, flung herself on top of him and began kissing and embracing him frantically, hysterically. He laughed weakly and returned her hugs as best he could.

"No time for that now," he said at last, when he had recovered breath enough to speak. "We must find the Ecolog." He grasped the claymore's handle and, with a grunt, pulled it free and returned it to the scabbard.

Garbage said with awe, "You killed a ngaa, with nothing but a sword."

Briggs shrugged. "Any creature that is hard on the outside is soft on the inside." He struggled to his feet, then leaned over to pick up the big rifle. He inspected the ammunition magazine. "Only one shot left in this blunderbuss," he mused. "Might come in handy."

Gun in hand, he started up the broad marble staircase, Garbage at his side.

In the throne room she said, "The Ecolog's not here. We'll never find her in this maze of a palace."

"I wouldn't be too sure about that." Briggs pointed to two trails of bloody footprints leading across the mosaic floor. "The Ecolog doesn't seem to realize it's not smart to step in a pool of blood before running off to hide."

They followed the trail to an apparently blank stone wall. Briggs knocked gently on the wall. It sounded hollow. "Stand back," he warned and aimed the gun.

The rifle's last bullet blasted a hole through the thin stone sheeting large enough for Briggs to squeeze through, and though it was no longer loaded, Briggs kept the gun as he and Garbage loped down the passage beyond the hole.

The trail of fading bloody footprints led them only 30 meters or so down a narrow passageway. Beyond that point lay a darkness so dense Briggs could hardly see his own hand, let alone a bootsole-shaped smudge of red.

But, since the passage appeared to have no branches, Briggs continued stubbornly groping his way along.

Garbage whispered, "Let me go first. I know the way." Brushing past him, she took the lead.

"You know? How?"

"I was one of the special girls. We all had to learn these passages."

Very soon she was dangerously far ahead of him. He struggled to catch up.

She called over her shoulder, "Here's where another secret panel opens out into the entrance hall near the big model of the galaxy."

Suddenly Briggs saw a light appear. She had opened the panel.

"Wait," called Briggs in a hoarse whisper, but Garbage ignored him and stepped through the opening.

An instant later Briggs heard her startled exclamation, "Klain!" followed by, "Briggs! Help!"

COMMODORE Briggs thrust his head through the opened panel. Garbage's call for help had ruined any chance for a surprise attack.

A few paces away he saw his little comrade, her face contorted with pain. Klain had twisted her arm behind her back and was holding a knife to her throat. The Ecolog was there too; she had changed her clothes and now wore the same simple, blue tunic and black high boots as her soldiers, though she retained her jeweled mask and curved sword. Briggs noted that she also had a stinger pistol stuffed in her belt; probably his own.

"Drop the rifle," Klain commanded.

Briggs hesitated a moment and said, "I think I'll keep it."

Klain smiled. "A standoff, eh? That's fine with me. Soon the Ecolog's guard will be along to cart you back where you belong."

Garbage cried out defiantly, "You think so? The Eco-log's guard has defected! All her troops have joined us."

Klain's gaunt features grew pale. "You're lying, Garbage Girl. You must think I'm stupid if you—"

The Ecolog cut in. "She's not lying. I know her. I know her as well as I know myself. Don't you think I could tell if she was lying?" Her voice rose, harsh and bitter. "It must be true! Of course it's true! Those fops and courte-sans, those toy soldiers . . . they all think they can rule better than me. This is their chance. Commodore Briggs is here to hold their hands, to give them courage, to prom-ise them the stars! Of course they've turned against me!" She glared at Briggs, blue eyes fierce and full of pain behind her slanted eyeslits. "Ah, my dear Commodore, if only you and I could fight, with this planet and every thing and every person on it as the prize. That's the way it is, you know. If I die you will have to rule this world yourself. Those spineless weaklings that follow you won't be able to command the respect of the masses. And if you die, all those turncoats will trample each other in their haste to return to me. You have nobody among your fol-lowers or crewmen who can take and hold a civilization."

Briggs listened and knew she was right.

Suddenly, behind him, Briggs heard excited voices.

The Ecolog laughed. "Not today, eh Commodore? The voters are coming!" She turned to Klain. "Follow me and bring the girl."

The excited voices were getting closer.

The Ecolog broke into a run, heading for the front exit.

Klain said, "Stand where you are, Briggs. This girl's life means nothing to me. By our laws she's already dead." He moved her arm upward; she went white with pain but re-fused to cry out.

Briggs decided to gamble. The heavy rifle was not loaded, but Klain didn't know that. Briggs raised the gun and pointed it at Klain and Garbage. He said softly, "Her life means nothing to me, either."

Briggs was thinking of how calmly Omen had murdered Lord Mayor Mano—that poor old fool—when Mano had been a hostage, and how everyone had regarded the murder as justified and normal. Abbututikan had strange customs, but Briggs was beginning to understand them. When Klain did not reply, Briggs added, "With this gun I can shoot you through her."

Briggs aimed directly at the girl's stomach and slowly began to squeeze the trigger. Garbage smiled faintly, as if to say, *At last you're learning.*

"Wait!" called out Klain. He released the girl and threw down his knife. Garbage ran to Briggs's side. Briggs handed her the gun, saying, "Keep him covered until the others get here." He could hear the voice of Mike Phillips in the distance and shouted, "This way, Mike!"

"Yes, sir," answered the distant voice.

Briggs left Klain and Garbage and ran toward the front exit. The Ecolog was not in sight, but she couldn't have gone far.

As he burst out into the courtyard, the sky was glowing with the first predawn light. Ahead of him the great bulk of the dirigible loomed.

But something was wrong!

The dirigible was in motion!

Someone had released the mooring cables and set it free. The faint breeze of early morning was enough to set it drifting silently toward the palace walls.

The propellers began to turn; their swish-swishing almost instantly became a roar of awesome power.

The airship began to rise.

CHAPTER 9

Trailing cables dangled from the bottom of the dirigible; Briggs remembered how expertly the airship crew had swung on them. One of the cables, Briggs noticed, was actually dragging on the ground.

He ran harder, head down like a charging bull, toward the trailing cable; his face was brick red, his breath came in strangled gasps. He felt dizzy, sick and old, but kept running anyway. The cable! Where was the cable? His vision blurred.

Then suddenly it was there, in sharp focus and so near he could almost grasp it. He leaped, caught it, felt himself jerked off his feet and pulled along the ground; then without warning, he was pulled violently upward, swinging toward the palace wall in a deadly arc that threatened to dash him against the stone.

He dragged himself upward on the cable.

The wall passed beneath him, so close he brushed it with his left heel. He reached the forward end of his swing and began to glide back like a living, kicking pendulum.

The outer wall of the palace passed below him, followed by a cliff, a sheer drop of at least half a kilometer. He was swinging in long, lazy ellipses now, the wind whipping his blue tunic, the thunder of the propellers deafening him. The cable was gnarled, not very slippery, but his fingers were already weakening, already beginning to ache. When he was younger, when he was rested, when he hadn't been out too long in the sun, he could have climbed this cable easily. But now it was torture.

The floor of the valley was far away. He could see a light fog down there in the shadow of the mountain, between the two ranges, and perhaps a glint of light on water . . . a river. There were trees, oh so distant. And jagged rocks.

167

Hand over hand, he began to climb the cable, slowly, painfully.

The dirigible began to descend. Abbututitikan was left behind, a white blob on the mountaintop, higher than Briggs. A lower mountain passed slowly below. The city of Arbre came into view but, except for a scattering of lights, was almost invisible in the shadow of the mountains.

Briggs climbed. His breath came in white puffs in the thin cold air. *Maybe that's why I'm so weak*, he thought. *The air's too thin at this altitude.*

Still he climbed.

His efforts had somehow started him rotating. He turned and turned, as if on an unstoppable spinning top. A terrible vertigo was growing in him. He was beginning to sweat; his hands were becoming slippery. The sky, as it rotated around him, was becoming steadily brighter.

He went on climbing. What else could he do?

He glanced up, and to his surprise saw that he was only a meter or so from the open deck at the rear of the gondola. He redoubled his efforts. But his hands began to slip, and he slid down a meter before he could stop himself.

Now blood was on his hands as well as sweat.

He began to climb again, more slowly and carefully.

This time he reached the edge of the deck, checked his spinning and hung there a moment gathering strength. Then, with one last mighty effort, he reached up, clutched one of the cold metal rods that served as part of the deck's inadequate guardrail and dragged himself, centimeter by agonizing centimeter, on board.

He rolled rather than crawled across the deck, coming to rest against the wall of the lounge. There he lay, panting and resting, waiting for his sickness and dizziness to pass, waiting for the Ecolog to come and kill him while he was helpless.

She did not come. She must not know he was here.

The propellers roared on. Dawn had fully broken now, and the sun was bright, making him squint.

When he recovered, he rose to his feet, drew his clay-more and cautiously entered the lounge.

No one was there.

Crouching, expecting an ambush, he started toward the forward end of the ship.

There was nobody in the games room, nobody in the dining hall, nobody in the galley. He entered the passenger area, began opening compartment doors, one at a time. All vacant.

He entered the cargo hold. The cargo hold was empty, without so much as a packing case to be seen. He retraced his steps, searched the lower passenger area. No one.

He was sure now. She must be in the pilot's compartment, at the controls, totally unaware that Briggs was on the ship.

He carefully opened the door to the radio room, made sure it was deserted and crept forward to the cockpit.

But it, too, was empty. A tiny red light indicated the ship was under control of the automatic pilot.

"Damn!" muttered Briggs. The Ecolog, it seemed, was not on the ship at all. She had set a trap, and he had fallen into it.

But never mind. With a little luck he could learn the controls and return to Abbututikan. He sheathed his sword and sat in the pilot's seat.

Suddenly, the red light went out, along with every other light on the instrument panel. Dumbfounded, Briggs stared at the dead panel as the propellers slowed to a swish-swish, before stopping altogether.

In the terrible silence Briggs looked around nervously.

Was the Ecolog here after all? Had she turned off the power from some place of concealment he'd missed? Or had she programed the ship to do this?

He glanced through the windows. The airship was coasting. It would probably continue to coast for hours, gradually losing altitude, until it settled . . . where? In the desert of course. There was nothing but desert to be seen down there, flat featureless desert, except for a small cloud of dust.

A pack of ngaas?

The ship creaked and groaned as the nose dropped slightly, but otherwise the only sound was the faint rushing of the wind. She was not on the ship, he decided. Why would she risk a crash landing in the desert if she was on the ship?

He glanced at the copilot's seat and froze.

There lay the stinger pistol, its ammunition clip removed. He sprang up, shouting, "You are on the ship! Where are you? Show yourself!"

From somewhere beyond the radio room he heard a peal of playful, triumphant contralto laughter.

HE still did not know where the Ecolog was, but he did know where she'd been. He'd found a small rectangular panel open above the cargo compartment. It led into the gasbag. Of course! The gasbag was not one big bag of helium, but many little bags with plenty of hiding places between them, places where there was no helium. Places where, no doubt, there were power switches.

Now she was somewhere in the gondola. Her laughter had seemed to come from somewhere aft.

He left the cargo compartment and started toward the rear.

He heard running footsteps; then silence again. Yes, she was back there all right. He realized she could easily have killed him, shot him in the back with the stinger pistol, but that was not her way. What she wanted, as she'd said plainly enough, was a duel to the death with the entire civilization of the planet as the prize.

So be it, thought Abraham Briggs. If only he wasn't so tired. . . .

Motionless, he listened; then he shambled aft, stopped and listened again. Was that a suppressed giggle? He couldn't be certain. Where did it come from?

He entered a hallway between two walls lined with doors that lead into passenger compartments. Although he'd already searched them once, she'd since moved. She could be behind any one of these silent closed doors, waiting for him.

"Must you play these silly games?" he shouted.

There was no answer.

He continued his search, checking each compartment again. All were deserted. He was weary, weary unto death. He wanted to shout, "I surrender!" A dozen times the words came to his lips, but he did not say them.

Slowly, carefully, he entered the dining hall.

"You said you wanted a duel," he shouted. "I'll give you a duel."

Silence.

Cautiously, he moved into the room, claymore at the ready.

Suddenly, without warning, he felt a sharp pain in his rear and spun around to face his attacker.

The Ecolog leaped back from her hiding place behind the serving counter. A few drops of blood were on the point of her curve-bladed, jewel-hilted scimitar.

"*Touché!*" she cried gleefully. "This is the second time I could have killed you."

"And the last," answered Briggs angrily, rubbing his backside. "*En garde!*"

He should have been ready, but he wasn't. Nobody could be ready for the sudden onslaught of perfectly executed lunges, digs, slashes and feints she now rained upon him, driving him steadily back through the room; chairs and tables were overturned in the haste of his awkward retreat. She was small and light, but awesomely quick; by contrast, he was a lumbering gorilla, barely able to fend off her blows.

Effortlessly, she cut him in the cheek, in the arm, in the leg, humming softly to herself some tune Briggs had never heard before but now would never forget.

He tried to stop her, at least slow her, but it was useless. She continued to drive him backward, never allowing him to find his balance, to dig in.

For an instant he thought he would have his back to the wall; but no, he found a doorway behind him and retreated through it. Was it luck or had she steered him to it? Was she herding him as a dog herds sheep?

He passed through the games room, the lounge, out the rear door onto the windy deck, always retreating. Suddenly she broke off and jumped back. For a moment the duel ceased.

"Where will you go now?" she asked softly.

Briggs knew without looking that nothing was behind him but a narrow metal guardrail and beyond that, emptiness. He sucked in great gulps of air, then admitted candidly, "I don't know."

"I know," said the Ecolog. "*En garde!*"

Briggs attacked first this time. She parried with a hit to the flat of his blade, easily sidestepping the cut, her blue eyes gleaming with delight. As Briggs recovered, she flashed the scimitar under his nose, forcing him to jump back, then followed up with a series of circular sweeping attacks as Briggs retreated, trying to use his longer blade and arm to hold her off.

Almost at the rail, he stop-thrusted to her head. She ducked under his sword, crouching with her left hand on the deck, and slashed at his belly, tearing through his tunic and leaving a painful gash. He brought his sword down but she rolled out of the way like an acrobat, landing on her feet in a low crouch.

Briggs followed through on his stroke, bringing the claymore around for another hit, but she sprang lightly back out of danger.

And the claymore swung down and struck the deck in front of her!

With a triumphant cry, she kicked the claymore from his hand, and as it scudded across the deck, she brought her blade swishing down for the final blow. In his move to avoid the slash, Briggs lost his balance and landed on his back.

Almost by reflex he raised his feet and caught her in the stomach. Her own momentum carried her into the air, her weight on his booted feet. He gave a little kick and she passed over him and struck the guardrail with a heavy crash and a cry of pain.

Her platinum mask fell off and bounced away.

As he tried to reach for her, she was rolling under the guardrail. He saw her face.

It was the face of the girl he called Garbage.

He clutched at her, in an attempt to save her, but she had already slipped over the edge.

As she fell she looked up into his eyes, completely unafraid, and he saw on her lips a faint, ironic smile.

He lay on his stomach on the deck and watched her until she finally hit the ground.

CHAPTER 10

"The planet is yours," said Captain Klain stiffly. "You have won it fairly, according to the terms set down by the Ecolog herself." His voice shook slightly, the only outward sign of the violent conflicting emotions Commodore Briggs knew must be raging inside the man.

"Thank you," said Briggs inadequately. He wished he could say more, wished he could find a way to make Klain his friend, but after all that had happened, it would be a long time before such a friendship was possible. "Thank you," he repeated.

Briggs and Klain shook hands formally, without warmth.

It was noon in Abbututikan. The sun was bright but the air was cool. A breeze was blowing, making work more difficult for the troops who were tying down the dirigible. Briggs had found the switch that turned on the power from the ship's nuclear pile and, after a few false starts, had piloted the airship home.

It was not a large group that stood there in the palace courtyard: Briggs, Klain, Lieutenant Phillips, the soldier Myron Marks, and the girl called Garbage. It was not a noisy group either. Nobody was cheering. Nobody was applauding. Even for Briggs and Phillips the death of the Ecolog left a curious vacuum, a painful sense of loss.

Briggs looked down at the gleaming metal object in his hands: the mask of the Ecolog. Its many-colored jewels sparkled in the sunlight no less brightly than they had sparkled when the Ecolog was alive.

With a sigh Briggs handed the girl the mask, saying, "This is yours, Garbage."

Unhesitatingly she took it and slipped it on. It fitted perfectly.

Briggs looked at her and said softly, "The Queen is dead. Long live the Queen."

Phillips, when he had recovered from his shock, protested, "You can't mean you intend to perpetuate the same form of government here as before! We could institute a parliamentary democracy, redistribute the wealth, free the people...."

Briggs shook his head slowly. "Not here, Mike. Not in this part of the galaxy."

"But why?" Mike persisted.

Briggs pointed toward the sun. "That looks like the sun that shines down on our own home Earth, but it's not. Ours is a population-one star, while this one is population-two, like all the stars outside the main disk of the galaxy. Within the main disk there can be democracy, widespread wealth, high technologies shared by the entire population, but not outside the main disk."

Mike exploded, "Nonsense! You're reading your own ultraconservative prejudices into the stars."

Briggs raised his voice. "You don't understand, Mike. Population-one stellar systems contain ample supplies of metal. Population-two systems contain almost none. Unless I am sadly mistaken, all the metal in this stellar system is contained in this one moonless planet, and nearly all the metal on this planet is here in Abbututikan. There's helium here in plenty—the continents are probably floating on pockets of helium big enough to supply fleets of dirigibles for eons—but there's only enough metal to supply one tiny oasis of high technology, Abututikan. For the rest of the world there's enough for a few swords and knives and essential tools, but that's all. I suspected something like this from the start, as soon as I saw we were outside the main galactic disk. When the cans we found in the abandoned city were plastic, I was sure of it."

Mike was stunned. "You knew all along...."

The commodore nodded wearily. "Something like the Ecolog was inevitable." He turned toward the soldier Myron. "Correct me if I'm wrong, sir, but I believe I've finally worked out the last few details, the things that I must admit I've not fully understood until now. The Ecolog is not really immortal, is she?"

Myron turned pale, but it was Klain who answered, almost inaudibly, "That's right."

Briggs pressed on. "She's not one person, but many."

"Not exactly," said Myron. "Every 40 years a new Ecolog puts on the mask, the mask that hides from the masses the signs of age. All the Ecologs are clones, all grown from bits of skin cut from the body of the original Ecolog, who brought our forefathers to this planet and founded this colony. Unfortunately the cloning process is not perfect. Each duplicate Ecolog is slightly different. Some have defects, major or minor, that do not show up at once. To get one perfect Ecolog, we must raise over 1,000 imperfect ones. The imperfect ones are called garbage girls and killed.

Briggs sighed, "Many are called, but one is chosen."

"That's right," said Myron. "Only one is allowed to reach the age of 22."

Mike was shaken. "It's a cruel system."

Briggs answered, "No more cruel than Mother Nature. The Ecolog has substituted human judgment for natural selection. It's survival of the fittest on a rational, scientific basis." His voice hardened. "But there is still one more secret. Myron, the original Ecolog is not altogether dead, is she?"

The soldier hesitated; then he said, "No, sir."

Klain looked up, startled. It seemed there were things even he did not know.

"Take me to her," Briggs commanded.

THE original Ecolog lay in a tank, eyes closed, perfectly still, not breathing, her heart not beating, yet she was not dead. Her bodily processes continued, but at such a slow pace they could not be detected without highly sensitive instruments. Briggs, looking down at her, recognized her state as one he'd seen back in India, on the home planet. Forms of autohypnosis were used there that could induce a deep trance more profound than hibernation—almost suspended animation. In such a state the processes of age were slowed too, almost to a standstill.

Briggs spoke softly, but his voice echoed in the dim, underground chamber. "I thought as much. You can't get living clones from dead tissue."

The woman in the tank was naked. Her body was covered with little scratches where bits of flesh had been taken for cloning. Each was marked by a tiny scab, but none of the scratches had completely healed; the trance slowed down the healing process as well.

Briggs noticed a metal band around the woman's forehead. (It was bizarre how perfectly she resembled an older Garbage . . . the same form and height, the same long blond hair.) "Can I communicate with her?" he asked, his eye tracing a wire that led from the metal band out of the tank and into a machine set in a niche above.

"Yes," said Myron, in a low voice.

He handed Briggs a similar metal band with a similar wire linking it to the machine. Briggs slipped it on over his head.

"Close your eyes to cut out distractions," instructed Myron.

Briggs closed his eyes.

Little by little he became aware of thoughts that were not his own, thoughts that had a finer, more delicate tone than any he was familiar with. Someone else was sharing his mind; a powerful, calculating intelligence that was nevertheless unmistakably feminine. Visions began to fade in and fade out, visions of things he had never seen, people he had never met. A small starship of ancient design and its crew of six men and six women, plus the womanly mind through whose eyes he watched them. A coven! He knew he was looking at the original colonists on their trip to this planet. Everyone who lived here was descended from this group of 12—or the Ecolog herself.

He saw a landing on a mountaintop and the construction of the first crude huts of Abbutututikan. There were dawns and noons and dusks. There was the formation and adjustment of an artificial Van Allen belt on the fringes of the atmosphere, the liberation of vast amounts of oxygen from the water in the seas and the gradual terraforming of the environment. There was the planting of seeds they'd brought with them and the destruction of native plant forms and the attempt, unsuccessful, to fill the new land with familiar animals.

It was all part of a plan, a billion-year plan. The Ecolog made the plan; then she slept. Her clones carried it out. Gradually Briggs became aware of a face. It was a face he had learned to call by the name Garbage.

A voiceless voice spoke softly to him.

I see you are a stranger.

Yes.

I see your name is Abraham.

Yes, said Briggs in his mind.

It is a meaningful name, Abraham. I see its meaning stretching into the shadows of the most distant past. It is not an easy name to wear, is it?

Sometimes it is hard. -

So is mine. I am the Ecolog. Our names are much alike. They both mean responsibility. Briggs felt cool blue eyes looking into him, seeing everything, rejecting nothing, judging nothing. He had always wanted someone to understand him, at the same time as he dreaded it. With awe and love, he watched the Ecolog become transparent to him, as he knew he was becoming transparent to her. He could sense it all; the great plan for the founding of a utopian civilization, the courage and determination to carry out the plan, the rush of images of an unhappy childhood, the half-hidden images of eating, tearing, rending, the animal subconscious, the hypnotic writhing of a stunted, frustrated eroticism. For a long time, there were no words. He and she stared into each other. That was enough.

At last she said, *I see you wish to use my master computer.*

Yes.

Upon the result of your computations depends the survival of my planet.

Yes.

Use my computer. I trust you with my world.

BRIGGS had been shaken by his wordless conversation more than he would ever admit. The Ecolog was behind him, in another room, no longer in communion with his innermost being; yet, in another sense, she would never be far from him again, as long as his memory continued to function.

The lights in this room were brighter, though the air was still cool with the coolness of a deep cave. The master computer stood before him, silent, dark, waiting.

After his communion, he had gone to the radio room of the dirigible and made radio contact with the *Corregidor.* The crew had been so hysterically glad to hear from him, particularly Christina Enge, yet he had not been able to respond fully to them. He was so tired. And the Ecolog had been so close to him that no one else would ever be as close.

They had radioed down the data for the computer.

He looked at the computer.

There was dust and spots of rust on it, and it was covered with the webs of the strange creatures that, on this planet, filled the ecological niche of spiders.

The girl called Garbage stood beside him. He glanced at her. She wore the mask of the Ecolog, but for him she was only a shadow of the real Ecolog, the silent body in the tank.

She said, "We haven't used this machine for 25 years."

He said, "Turn it on."

She touched the stud. Banks of lights snapped to life, began to blink out their coded signals. A soft hum began to drone from behind the gray metal panels.

The rust and the dust worried him somewhat but there was little he could do about it.

He shrugged. In his hand was a plastic card banded with strips of bonded germanium. Each separate atom in the germanium bands was able to hold a simple code. Yes or no. Off or on. And out of this multitude of separate positives and negatives could be built any mathematical process known to man.

His hand was sweating slightly as he placed the card in the computer's read unit.

It was the new Ecolog who pressed the stud for "Program Start."

In a single flash the card was read. The computer began its deliberations with only a few changes in the pattern of flashing lights, changes only an expert could notice, let alone interpret.

Side by side Briggs and the new Ecolog awaited the answer. He took her hand. They watched the screen where the answer would first appear, an instant before the print-out unit would begin to record it.

Briggs expected a simple answer.

Would the star take an energy tap large enough to refuel the Corregidor? Or would it explode?

The screen lit up. Briggs began to read.

"BLKJHGFD IUYT MNV"

"What does that mean?" demanded the Ecolog.

Briggs's voice was worried. "Nothing at all."

"Maybe it needs a minute to settle down to business," she said.

The computer said, "45 68 BCHFXXR WQ) (*&¢% "

Briggs smelled ozone, heard the telltale crackle of electricity arcing. His hand darted toward the "Program Stop" stud, but the computer beat him to it. Every light on the panel went out at once. A thin wisp of smoke curled up from under the read unit. The computer was dead.

"Can it be repaired?" demanded Briggs.

She shook her head. "We no longer have anyone who knows how."

"Maybe someone from the *Corregidor*. . . ." Briggs had located the snaps that released the easy access panel. He unsnapped them, opened up the machine and peered inside.

The individual modules were intact, but the problem lay with the insulated wires leading from one module to another. The insulation was almost all gone. On closer examination, Briggs could see a horde of tiny insects contentedly chewing on what insulation remained. He watched them for a long time, thinking about all the pain and hardship, all the struggle and loss of life that had brought him to this moment. All, all for nothing.

He sighed and replaced the panel.

"What are you going to do now?" demanded the Ecolog. There was a kind of faith in her voice, a certainty that even now Briggs was not defeated, that even now he would have some new ingenious scheme. From behind her eyeslits, her blue eyes peered at him expectantly.

He returned her gaze, thinking of all he had gone through with her, thinking of the other Ecologs: the one who'd tried to kill him, the one in the tank who'd been, for a few minutes, like his second self.

"What are you going to do now?" she repeated, more sharply.

"Abandon and destroy the *Corregidor*. If I'm not imposing, I'd like permission for my crew and myself to live the rest of our lives on your planet." His voice was flat and toneless.

NUMBLY, as if in a dream, Commodore Briggs stood at the porthole in the *Corregidor*'s secondary control room, his feet held to the deck by magnetic boots, watching the *Manta One* dwindle to a dot silhouetted against the glowing half-sphere of the planet's dayside. The little shuttlecraft had been retrieved by remote control as soon as the Ecolog's power-jammer had been turned off, only to be pressed into service for the sad task of transporting the crew, in groups of ten, down to the surface. The other shuttleships were being readied for the same purpose.

At his side stood the new Ecolog.

The mask of authority had transformed her. The fearful fugitive he had met in the abandoned city had vanished without a trace. She was now truly a queen; her every movement, the very way she stood showed it. Briggs wondered idly, *Which is her real self? Her innermost consciousness or the role she plays in her society?*

It was one of those somewhat profound, philosophical questions that can't be answered, yet which are the foundation of our whole way of understanding reality. If it was her role that was her real self, then the Ecolog was indeed as immortal as she pretended. If it was her innermost self, then her immortality was a fraud.

"Dutton," called Briggs.

"Yes, sir," answered the chief engineer, seated at the nearby control console. The man seemed to have aged in the past few days. His thin face was more lined than Briggs remembered it, his crew-cut hair even grayer.

"Take over the helm," said Briggs.

"Aye, sir," said Dutton, still the by-the-book officer he'd always been. Dutton, perhaps, was one of the lucky ones who were the same inside as outside. Or maybe he wasn't. Briggs watched the man intently for a moment, wondering if he wasn't, after all these years of shared service, still a stranger.

"Come along," said Briggs to the Ecolog.

He led her to his cabin, where he began to open his drawers and stuff his few belongings into his dufflebag and foot locker. It was a comical undertaking in zero gravity, where a sock or pair of shorts might escape and drift across the room. The Ecolog laughed at his antics, and he laughed too, but she did not pitch in and help him. She had her dignity to think of.

He found a picture of himself in his gaudy graduation uniform, taken on the day he'd gotten his sheepskin at New Annapolis.

The Ecolog said softly, "That's you, isn't it?"

He nodded slowly. "Yes, when I was young, just starting out. Now I'm old and finished."

"No, no, don't say that. There is work for you in Abbututikan. A whole new career! You can be to me what Klain was to my predecessor."

"I don't know if that's possible. The ways of your court are strange. Your civilization has greatly diverged from the rest of humanity. I don't know if I could go along with your monopoly on knowledge, though I see the reasoning behind it, or if I could accept the wholesale slaughter of what you call the 'special girls.' "

She rested her hand on his arm, saying, "We'll change all that. I was planning to anyway. It's the only means I can see for arresting our society's slow slide into oblivion. The people will be taught! I promise you that. And the special girls will no longer be killed, but given useful work to do out among the people. I need you here to give me new ideas, to guide me and my colony back into the mainstream of mankind."

He sighed. "Yes, perhaps it will work out. But it isn't a starship. It isn't leaping from planet to planet down the arms of the nebula. It isn't facing danger and winning. Winning has always been important to me, my dear. Mike Phillips thinks it's an unhealthy obsession, a sign of my basic insecurity, my need to constantly prove myself. It may be that he's right, and that what I've needed all my life and been unconsciously searching for is one really crushing defeat, one resounding failure. If I can survive it and come out on the other side, I won't be afraid of failure any more. Failure will be my friend." His voice had gradually grown more bitter.

She took his sullen face in her delicate hands and turned it toward her. She said, "There is no defeat until you surrender. You have not surrendered, only shifted to a new battlefield."

"Let me see your face."

"All right."

He removed her mask, put his great bearlike arms around her. She kissed him tenderly on the lips. He returned the kiss, feeling the terrible tension of the last few days begin to drain away. He wanted to cry, but could not.

Their lips parted. He could feel her warm breath on his cheek as she whispered, "You see? You'll be as much a giant here as anywhere. You'll always be a giant, no matter where you are."

They were both startled by a raucous bleep on the intercom. Chief Engineer Dutton's voice blatted out at them. "Commodore Briggs! We've just picked up a message on tight laser from the planet's surface. Ground station telescopes have spotted two Lorn starships on the other side of the globe. They're decelerating to make orbit."

The commodore hesitated only an instant before giving his command. "Discontinue disembarkation. Make the stellar tap. We're going to fight 'em!"

Roughly, he pulled himself free from her arms and dove for the door.

CHAPTER 11

The process was swift. As the gravatic shifter tapped into the raw energy of the nearby star, the *Corregidor* came back to life. The lights burned brighter. The intercom—which now barked orders from Dutton—sounded louder. The artificial gravity returned and quickly built up to a full one G, making his steps firm as Briggs strode toward the secondary control room. He could hear the Ecolog's running footsteps behind him, but he paid no attention.

By the time he reached the room, the tap had been completed. Mike Phillips, Dutton, Hughes and DeCarli were strapped in their seats, looking up through the canopy at the sun.

Phillips saw Briggs and said, "The supernova. . . ." He was pale and shocked.

Briggs snapped, "All it can do is kill us, and that's no worse than what the Lorns have planned. Now get this ship moving! The Lorns won't wait!"

As he strapped himself into his seat, Briggs saw the Ecolog framed in the doorway. Her mask was still off, clutched in her hand, and her face was filled with a horrified dawning understanding of what was going on around her.

"You're going to blow up the sun!" she shouted.

Briggs answered, "Find a seat! Strap down!"

The rising whine of power indicated the drive had been engaged, but the stasis field prevented it from being felt. Above the canopy the sun swung out of view and the Magellanic Clouds—two fuzzy balls of stars—appeared. The ship was accelerating rapidly as it swung from the dayside to the nightside of the planet. The room darkened as they entered the planetary shadow. The Great Whirlpool came in sight, filling the sky.

The Ecolog was still standing, eyes round with shock.

185

The Lorns might or might not know he was here. They certainly would not expect him to attack against such odds. This time the element of surprise was in Briggs's favor.

"There they are," said Dutton.

Two dots of light had appeared on the viewscreen, moving against the background of the galaxy.

"Hit them," Briggs whispered.

Dutton gestured over the firing stud. The forward shifters hummed. A portion of the energy so recently drawn from the sun was shifted on a gravatic carrier wave to the first of the Lorn starships.

"She's badly damaged, sir," said Dutton.

"Hit again!" said Briggs.

The second energy shift must have reached the Lorns' own energy banks. There was a brief, brilliant flash, totally silent in the void.

"Nothing but an expanding globe of debris," reported Dutton.

"Good," said Briggs.

"But the other Lorn is taking evasive action."

"Hit him!"

"Missed."

"I'll take the controls."

"Yes, sir."

Briggs's fingers danced over the studs of the control console as if he were some sort of demonic concert pianist playing a concerto no one could hear. He felt a savage exhilaration that burned away all weakness, cleared his mind, banished weariness, made him feel young again.

The Lorn ship was large enough on the viewscreen so he could make out its structure quite clearly as, a moment later, it emerged from the planetary shadow into the sunlight. Abruptly the *Corregidor*, too, emerged from the shadow.

There was the sun, the same as always. The *Corregidor* had fallen into an attitude that made the sun shine directly down into the secondary control room through the canopy, which instantly changed color to protect them from too bright a light.

The Ecolog cried out, "The sun! It didn't explode!"

But Briggs was only dimly aware of her presence as he concentrated on his task.

Now the *Corregidor* and the Lorn ship were darting about like angry waterbugs, firing and running, firing and running. They were unusually close for a space battle, yet Briggs kept pressing in, narrowing the already narrow range.

The Lorn ship started to make a run for it.

In the split second before it reached top speed, Briggs nailed it.

It exploded in a brilliant, silent blaze of light.

All around him the crew went wild, leaping up and dancing and cheering, but Briggs remained in his chair, breathing heavily, finally whispering a single word.

"Beautiful."

As if waking from a trance, he blinked and looked around him. He frowned. The Ecolog had gone. He unstrapped himself.

Lurching to his feet, he lumbered from the control room in search of her. Dutton, glancing after him, took over the controls.

HE searched for some time, asking questions, drawing surprised stares, occasionally barking into the intercom either an order for the resumption of normal operations or an inquiry about the Ecolog's whereabouts.

It was Chaplain Ellington who found her and called him. "She's here in the *Manta* launching chamber, Commodore, requesting transportation down to Abbutututikan."

"Hold her there."

Briggs hurried aft.

The Ecolog had donned her mask of office. She stood in the open air lock of *Manta Four,* straight and proud in blue tunic and black boots.

She said, "It's time to go to work, Commodore." Her voice was calm, faintly amused.

He stared at her a moment in silence. Awkwardly, he began, "I'm sorry. I can't go with you now. You see—"

She said softly, playfully, "You love them more than me."

"Who?" Briggs was thinking of the service, the fleet.

"The Lorns."

She stepped through the air lock.

It closed between them.

Briggs left the launching chamber and gave the command himself, "On the count of three. One, two, three." The air that escaped with the *Manta* sounded curiously like a sigh.

Through a porthole, Briggs watched the *Manta* descend. Chaplain Ellington stood nearby but did not disturb him. It was Dutton on the intercom who at last broke into his reverie.

"Your orders, Commodore?"

"Eh? What's that? Yes, I want all hands to shuttle up to the ship, then we're heading back for the war zone. I'll navigate."

Dr. Christina Enge entered the room. "I see you're feeling better, Commodore," she said.

He glanced at her. "Yes, Doctor. I'm quite recovered."

She said, "You had it all figured out, didn't you? Almost from the start."

He nodded. "As soon as I heard those voices on the radio speaking English, the picture was fairly clear. I was sure the people on this planet must have come from Earth or one of Earth's colonies. There are limits to the principle of parallel development, you see; it's impossible for exactly the same language to evolve independently on two different planets. That was my reasoning, and it's turned out I was right."

"But this is so far outside the borders of the known universe!" she exclaimed.

"Yes, and that fact supplied me with another part of the puzzle. Before we encountered the Lorns, the universe was not thought to have borders. Borders are the result of war, and the Lorns were the first race we met that presented a genuine challenge. It may seem strange, but early in the age of space, at the time of the massive interstellar migrations, human colonists flew off in all directions and kept going until they found something they liked. If they never returned, it was assumed they'd either found a place for themselves or perished. No one kept records or tried to map it all. Those were wild days, Doctor! I thought it safe to assume this planet was one of the colonies founded way back then. Today nobody would dare establish themselves so far away from the rest of humanity."

He stared out the porthole a while in silence; then he said softly, "The age of expansion is over for them down there, and for us too. Future historians may call our era the age of contraction. Living organisms don't take well to contraction, or to standing still. Growth is life! Mankind would have become extinct, you know, if we hadn't learned how to escape the Earth. Earth was well on the way to becoming the same as that unfortunate planet down there." He gestured toward the cloud-covered ball beyond the porthole. "We owe the survival of our whole species to those few individuals who made it possible for us to expand into space before it was too late, before the level of natural resources dropped too low for space technology to function. It was touch and go around the end of the twentieth century! A few more years would have made the difference between the star-voyaging creatures we are and the dwindling, defeated creatures we might have been. Make no mistake, mounting shortages would have forced a totalitarian regime on us; we would have had our own Ecolog, or someone very much like her, before the end."

She studied his somber face. "Do you think, Commodore, we will ever have another age of expansion?"

"If we beat the Lorns, yes."

She touched his arm. "What a grim prospect! Must it be a . . . a fight to the death?"

"I'm afraid so."

"But there's a moral question here. Do we have the right to wipe out a whole species?" Her tone was quiet, but contained an undercurrent of urgency. "Tell me, will we be right if we do that?"

Briggs smiled faintly. "As Ambrose Bierce put it, war is not fought to determine who is right, but who is left."

TEN hours later, all hands on board, the *Corregidor* broke orbit and accelerated rapidly. Commodore Abraham Briggs left the secondary bridge and, humming softly to himself, began a careful inspection of the weapons systems.

www.ingramcontent.com/pod-product-compliance
Lightning Source LLC
Chambersburg PA
CBHW050735250626
47155CB00005B/1784